The Amish Nurse Series #3

Playing on the Outhouse Roof

Stephanie Schwartz

Contents

PLAYING ON THE OUTHOUSE ROOF
Copyright © 2023 by Stephanie Schwartz

ISBN: 979-8-88653-150-3

Published by Satin Romance
An Imprint of Melange Books, LLC
White Bear Lake, MN 55110
www.satinromance.com

Published in the United States of America.

Cover Design by Caroline Andrus
Interior Illustrations: by Alexsi Currier
Permission given for all illustrations.
Permission to quote *The Budget* newspaper given by its editor, Milo G. Miller and the author of *Neither Wolf Nor Dog,* Kent Nerburn.

From Time Will Tell

THE AMISH NURSE SERIES, BOOK #2

Stephen and Phoebe had just gotten back from seeing Roberta, their midwife. He had taken a couple of hours off, leaving the furniture barn in his apprentice's Levi's care right after lunch. There was more than enough to do that he could easily handle without Stephen looking over his shoulder every minute. Tools needed cleaning and oiling, the suction system needed emptying of all its sawdust, the floors could use a good sweep and a multitude of other tasks would keep him out of trouble.

Roberta had Phoebe lie down on the exam table and measured her stomach from top to bottom with a paper measuring tape. Then she felt her stomach, 'walking' her fingers around using her fingertips where she expected the baby to be settled snug inside her bag of waters. Then she took the paper measuring tape once again and measured Phoebe's stomach from side to side this time. Neither Stephen nor Phoebe noticed Roberta's puzzled look quite yet.

"Hang in there while I go get the Doppler," Roberta said as she hurriedly left the exam room. She returned shortly and squirted the conducting gel onto the machine's wand before running it slowly across the expanding belly. The instrument crackled for a bit until she came to the spot she was looking for and came to rest there. They could all hear the slow faint, blub, blub, blub sound then.

"That's your heartbeat," Roberta explained to the couple. Moving the wand further down they could instantly hear a much faster, blub, blub sound.

"And that's your baby," she explained.

"It sounds more like a pony, than a baby in there," Stephen laughed, squeezing his wife's hand that he had been already holding.

Then moving the wand back up the growing mound of her belly, Roberta brought it to rest once again at another point. Immediately the Doppler picked up the fast blub, blub, blub sounds.

"And that is your other baby," Roberta said, trying to keep a straight face. No one spoke as the Doppler continued to amplify this heartbeat around the room. Stephen looked at Phoebe, who looked at Roberta and then back to Stephen. They continued to try to take in this new revelation but appeared unable to do so. Shock can do that to a person. They were both rendered speechless. Suddenly Phoebe burst into tears. Stephen took both her hands in his. All he could say was, "Are you sure? You're really sure? *Really?*" Stephen begged Roberta.

"Yes, I am sure. I started suspecting it when I saw how wide your tummy was getting," she said with a huge smile. "And now they are old enough at fifteen weeks to confirm with the Doppler. Congratulations!"

Glossary *

Ach!—Plain expression meaning "Oh!"

Amische—Pennsylvania Dutch dialect word meaning "The Amish."

Ausbund—The German *hymnal* containing centuries-old songs used by Amish and other Anabaptist peoples.

Basel—Hutterish word meaning "Hutterite woman."

Beheef dich—Pennsylvania Dutch dialect phrase meaning "behave, you."

Bobbel—Pennsylvania Dutch dialect word meaning "baby" (singular.)

Bobbeli—Pennsylvania Dutch dialect word meaning "babies" (plural.)

Boova—Pennsylvania Dutch dialect word meaning "boys" (plural.)

Dat—Pennsylvania Dutch dialect word referring to or addressing one's father.

Dawdi haus—Pennsylvania Dutch dialect word meaning "a grandparents' apartment usually attached to a main house."

Denke—Pennsylvania Dutch dialect word meaning "thank you."

Die boova sin do—Pennsylvania Dutch dialect phrase meaning "the boys are here."

Die gute schtup—Pennsylvania Dutch dialect word meaning "the living room" or "great room."

Dindla—Hutterish word meaning "little girl," affectionate.

Do net—Pennsylvania Dutch dialect word meaning "do not" or "don't."

Doddy—Pennsylvania Dutch dialect word meaning or when addressing one's "grandfather."

Englische(rs)—Pennsylvania Dutch dialect general term meaning "non-Amish" (plural.)

Erschtaunlich—Pennsylvania Dutch dialect word meaning "astonishing."

Es gschwall—Pennsylvania Dutch dialect word meaning "the squirrels" (plural.)

Fastnachts—Mennonite expression meaning "fried donuts."

Ferhoodled—Pennsylvania Dutch dialect word meaning "mixed up, flummoxed."

Frau(s)—Pennsylvania Dutch dialect word meaning "wife/wives," (plural).

Gay—Pennsylvania Dutch dialect command directing a horse to "walk on" or "giddy-yap."

Gut—Pennsylvania Dutch dialect word meaning "good."

Gott—Pennsylvania Dutch dialect word meaning "God."

Grossmammi—Pennsylvania Dutch dialect word meaning or addressing one's "grandmother."

'Hof—Hutterish/Tyrolean word shortened from Bruderhof meaning the 'Place of the Brothers.'

Kapp—Pennsylvania Dutch dialect word meaning "prayer cap/bonnet."

Kavli—Pennsylvania Dutch dialect word meaning "Amish double handled covered diaper basket."

Kesslehaus—Pennsylvania Dutch dialect word meaning "wash house."

Kinner—Pennsylvania Dutch dialect word meaning "children" (plural.)

Kumm—Pennsylvania Dutch dialect word meaning "come."

Leut—Pennsylvania Dutch and German word meaning "the (gathered) people" of a specific church.

Liedersammlung—A collection of German songs used by many Amish congregations.

Mamm—Pennsylvania Dutch dialect word to address one's "mother, mom."

Mammi—Pennsylvania Dutch dialect word meaning "grandma" (familiar.)

Mann—Pennsylvania Dutch dialect word usually meaning "husband."

Maud—Pennsylvania Dutch dialect word meaning "maid" often hired, or "unmarried older woman."

Meedel—Pennsylvania Dutch dialect word meaning "girls" (plural.)

Mudder—Hutterish word for "mother."

Ol' vetter—Hutterish word for "old man" and "grandfather."

Oma—German word for "grandma."

Opa—German word for "grandpa."

Ordnung—Plain word used by both Hutterites, Amish and Mennonites and other Anabaptist churches meaning "the written and unwritten rules and traditions of the Plain communities."

Patties—'Patties down,' Pennsylvania Dutch dialect word meaning "hands down" as in prayer, instructing children.

Rivvel(s)—Pennsylvania Dutch dialect word meaning "tiny soup dumplings made by grating dough into boiling broth" (plural.)

Rumschpringe—Pennsylvania Dutch dialect word literally meaning "running around," a time allowed in Amish youths' teen years before committing to the church through believers' baptism.

Schnapps—Taken from the German, word meaning "liquor" or "whiskey."

Shnitz—Pennsylvania Dutch dialect word meaning "dried apple."

Sits ana—Pennsylvania Dutch dialect word meaning "(please) sit down."

Schtruvel(s)—Pennsylvania Dutch dialect word meaning "loose hair(s)" (plural.)

Schwester—Pennsylvania Dutch dialect word meaning "sister."

Tract – Plain word found in Pennsylvania Dutch and Hutterish meaning "religious clothing."

Vetter—Hutterish word meaning "man/men" (singular and plural).

Wunderbar-gut—Pennsylvania Dutch dialect word meaning "wonderful" and "good."

Ya—Pennsylvania Dutch dialect word meaning "yes."

Yo—Pennsylvania Dutch dialect word meaning "yes" or "hey..."

Youngie—Pennsylvania Dutch dialect word meaning "the youth."

Ztzvilling—Pennsylvania Dutch dialect word meaning "twins."

* Although I have tried to represent Pennsylvania Dutch, German, and Hutterish throughout my books as accurately as I can, I am sure my readers who are native speakers will always be able to find fault for which I sincerely ask forgiveness. I know I will never get it perfect, but I hope you will allow for this. Thank you!

Part One

CHAPTER 1
Phoebe

"I can't believe it! I just don't believe it," Phoebe sobbed.

"Well, they say, 'be careful what you wish for,'" Stephen reminded her, shaking his head, still finding this news incredulous.

"I just can't believe we're really having *ztzvilling!*" Phoebe sniffed as she took a tissue Roberta offered while she carefully wiped the gel off of Phoebe's stomach with a washcloth. "You can sit up now," Roberta told her.

"There are a few things we'll have to talk about now," Roberta began as Phoebe settled herself upright on the end of the exam table, fussing with her apron that remained twisted around her knees, Stephen at her side holding her *kapp* in his hands that had fallen off when she laid back on the table.

"First, I cannot be your primary provider after this. You are now considered a high-risk pregnancy with twins. Midwives can only attend low-risk births, but I can still be with you in the hospital."

"Oh no," Phoebe said and promptly started crying all over again.

"Well, the good news is that we have a doctor at the hospital in Hudson who might help you have your twins naturally. He's pretty radical and has had very good success. It's only one and a half hours from here. That's plenty of time for a first baby. You can see our doctor here in the clinic for your checkups, and you and I can still visit. We'll make an appointment with him before you leave today, okay? Now that's enough for one day. Go home and celebrate. You don't drink champagne, do you?"

"No," Phoebe sniffed, still gulping between breaths as she pinned her *kapp* back in place. "We'll make hot cocoa, for sure," she said, while trying to slip off the end of the table and onto the floor. Stephen took her hand and helped her, saying, "I can't believe it. Wow. There aren't any twins in my family for as far back as I can think. How about yours?" he asked Phoebe.

"No, I don't remember hearing about any at all. We'll have to ask *Mamm.*"

They sat in silence on the way home in the buggy, each trying to take in this unexpected turn of events. Phoebe was glad for the padded bench as the buggy rocked along the road. Their horse fell into her usual slow-paced clip-clop on the shoulder of the road toward home, the metal wheel rims scratching along on the macadam. At dusk there weren't many cars on the country lane. Stephen had turned on the battery powered Coleman lantern hanging from the back corner of the roof on the buggy to alert cars should one come by. Corn fields framed the horizons all around them as the road wound through the area. The last rays sunbathed the tips of the corn tassels in a pinkish glow before it would disappear completely. A dog barked off in the distance as they neared *Dat's* farm.

Would their lives ever be dull again, like they were before they met at the singing over a year ago? *We were so, so utterly naïve, weren't we?* Phoebe asked herself. *And such a lack of faith, fretting all those long years back then (seven years plus three months and five days to be exact, but who was counting?) I thought I would be an old* maud *for certain and was sure the bishops had* kumm *to the house so unexpectedly to ask me to marry some old widower off in some God-forsaken outback* who had ten kinner—*at least*—"*You'll be doing such a* gut *service for the church* schwester...." Oh, *if only we trusted more that* Gott *would find the perfect life for each one of us if only we were prayerful and obedient to His word. We for sure make life complicated for ourselves, eh?*

At the same time, Stephen was pondering along the same lines. *I was convinced I was cut out to be a bachelor for the rest of my life. By thirty you give up, though I never really dated. I didn't want to be all disappointed, I guess, so I never really hoped. I think I left it up to* Gott *to decide and spare myself all the drama I saw when fellows tried to control it all. Some make some pretty bad mistakes picking out the prettiest girl and not considering if they are* Gott-*fearing and not just shallow or not quite mature yet. Then they are stuck for the rest of their lives with their choice. I wouldn't want that either. But why me? Why have You blessed us and not the others, like my own brother, for example? And now twins? You sure have a sense of humor,* Gott. *A double whammy. Whatever next? No, I don't wanna know, actually.* "Erschtaunlich!" he said under his breath.

Phoebe's musings brought her back to that moment again when she first met Stephen as the horse clip-clopped along while the Coleman lantern swung back and forth from where it was suspended, squeaking slightly with the rhythm of the buggy. The horse turned into the long gravel drive without being prodded. She could carry them home with her eyes closed. She had done it so many times.

I'll never forget the first time I saw Stephen, I mean really saw him, not just with a bunch of guys at church trying to keep their eyes open for three hours through those sermons that dragged on and on, glued to a backless bench in someone's barn on a sweltering hot day. He was so... so beautiful. He was. Young, fresh, eager, so full of life. So warm and friendly. And then he asks me to ride home with him to top it off! I'd completely forgotten about the custom. With school, I'd forgotten about the whole dating scene. Totally forgot what should have been my 'running around' years. I guess with college I'd given up rumschpringe *altogether. And on that first buggy ride home, I thought I'd faint. Even in the dark, maybe more in the dark, his voice, his beautiful rich, honest voice. There was nothing trying to impress. Only genuine friendship. But then I told him I couldn't see him again until I'd graduated, that I couldn't get distracted and end up disappointing the bishops who'd asked me to go to the nursing program. I just couldn't. Even then, I dreamt about him. Holding hands, waking up feeling the thrill of it still.*

So he writes me letters, such a determined brother. Sweet letters, but stupid me. I didn't even write back, as I was so afraid of getting off track, and I knew he'd probably meet someone else, but I really couldn't risk everything I had committed to already. I couldn't see my way through. I should have prayed more, not just decided on my own, that was it. 'Oh, ye of little faith'... she continued to think.

They finally got home in time for supper. After settling the horse in the barn, leading her out of the shafts and harness and rubbing her coat down, Phoebe made sure there was feed in the stable box while Stephen checked the water trough. She wasn't ready to go into the house they shared with her parents just yet. Better to wait for Stephen. She shivered then, leaning against the barn door, pulling her wool shawl tighter as she watched the sun slip below the tree line on the far horizon. Just then, she felt a new sensation in the depths of her body. A butterfly? Or was she just hungry? No, there it was again. Life. New life. A baby. A real live baby. A kick. What miracle! What wonder! Her heart expanded to the outer universe. What love.

They closed up the barn and walked up to the house, stumbling into the kitchen through the dark mudroom where they hung their coats and her travelling bonnet on the wall pegs there and left their shoes on the rag rug. The lamps were lit above the table and by the stove, leaving the corners of the room in shadows. The blue curtains had been pulled shut. The room was warm and smelled heavenly. The table was already set with a fresh blue checkered tablecloth. Four places were neatly laid out with mugs for coffee or tea with dessert. A large, covered Corning Ware casserole was sitting on a mat in the center of the table. A basket of fresh sliced brown bread and a dish of butter were arranged further down. A small bowl of homemade pickles and a jar of apple butter with a spoon stuck into it completed the menu.

Dat was sitting at the head of the table reading *The Budget,* which he began folding up as they hung their coats in the mudroom. In the buggy, they had agreed to wait until dessert to break the news to *Mamm* and *Dat*.

"That smells *wunderbar-gut, Mamm*. What is it?" Phoebe asked.

"I made that seven-layer deep dish *Dat* likes so well. *Ya* know, the one with sausage, rice, peas, potatoes and onions and carrots and tomato soup," *Mamm* said, and then looking at Stephen she added, "but there's no green peppers in it this time. I left it out."

"Denke," he replied, smiling. "That's *gut*. It smells *wunderbar*. I'm hungry."

They all enjoyed a leisurely supper chatting about this and that and the auction coming up on the weekend when *Dat* would go just to keep up on the price of cows and pigs and catch up with some of his *Amische* neighbors. He invited Stephen to come along so they could visit in the buggy. They both worked so hard all week they seldom found time to visit.

"Are you *kumming* too, *Mamm?*" *Dat* asked.

"No," she answered after gulping down her last bite. "I'm thinking of making up a bunch of cereal this weekend to have for the winter. Maybe a few gallons of grape nuts, a couple of jars of that homemade cereal with the rice cereal, and a bunch of home-made granola. I got all the fixings at the co-op last week. I'll make enough for the boys' families, and yours too, Phoebe. They'll enjoy that," *Mamm* said. "You can help if you have time, Phoebe."

"I'd like that," she answered absentmindedly, still thinking about the visit with the midwife. She jumped up and started clearing away the plates.

"I've got some dessert," *Mamm* announced, "so keep your forks."

Mamm proudly brought the pie to the table with four dessert plates, the pie server, and a knife.

"I made buttermilk pie. Hope you like it," she said as she cut into it. Stephen reached for Phoebe's hand under the table, signaling that the time had come. They couldn't avoid it any longer.

"Well," Stephen began after they were all served. "We saw the midwife today."

Mamm set the knife down and looked at both of them, squinting slightly, and frowning. It suddenly seemed to register that they were more worried about this conversation than she'd expected.

"Nothing's wrong, is it? You two look mighty serious. Is it? Is there something wrong with the baby?" she said, her voice inching up a decibel.

Trying to keep a straight face, Stephen informed them, "No, there's nothing wrong with the babies." Then he let that bit of information sink in. A long moment of quiet followed. *Mamm* blinked, looked at Phoebe, then at *Dat,* and back to Stephen again. Finally, Phoebe broke the silence.

"We found out it's twins, *Mamm,*" she announced as she teared up once again, reaching into her skirt waist for the handkerchief she had tucked there. *Mamm* was dumbstruck. *Dat* was the next to speak.

"Well, well. Isn't that something?" he stated plainly, a huge grin expanding above his salt and pepper beard, which he stroked as he contemplated this news.

"Is she sure? I mean, how can she even tell this early?" *Mamm* wanted to know as she laid down the pie server and sat back down.

Stephen explained. "We heard the two heart beats today. They have an instrument that amplifies it into the room so we could both hear them. It's pretty amazing. I mean that, and also thinking we'll have two babies—for the price of one, actually. I'm not quite used to the idea yet, to be honest."

"Oh, my goodness," *Mamm* gushed, jumping up and hugging first Phoebe and then Stephen. Then *Dat* reached over and shook Stephen's hand, congratulating him.

"Are you two happy? You seem a bit concerned," *Mamm* asked then.

Phoebe answered her while still daubing at her eyes. "Well, it changes some things. We can't have a home birth, but the hospital in Hudson has a doctor who is pretty *gut* with natural twin births. And I have to gain a whole lot more weight and try to slow down at the end, so they don't *kumm* early, things like that. We haven't really figured it all out, but I guess my dream has *kumm* true. Gosh. I still don't believe it. Neither of us can." *I just hope I don't regret wishing all that down the road,* she suddenly thought to herself.

"We will have to *kumm* up with two names, then. Maybe Zeke and Zack?" Stephen asked and began chuckling, leaning back in his chair. With a shocked look suddenly coming over his face, he sat up straight, loudly hitting the floor with the front two chair legs and said, "Oh, no! I'll have to make a 'nother whole cradle!"

"Or Romeo and Juliet?" Phoebe asked to which *Dat* and Stephen groaned simultaneously.

"Dick and Jane would be cute if you have one of each," *Mamm* offered, attempting to be helpful. "Or Jacob and Rachel?"

Then *Dat* suggested, "How 'bout Tweedle Dee and Tweedle Dum," and laughed out loud.

"Let's just enjoy our pie," Phoebe said dryly. This was going from bad to worse. "The world will never feel the same, I'm afraid. Who would have guessed?" she added as she cut into the creamy pie.

Then *Dat* asked, "What are the chances of it being triplets?" As he said it, he saw Stephen visibly grow pale right before his very eyes.

"Well, I looked it up once at school," Phoebe began, swallowing her first forkful, "and twins are born about thirty-seven times out of every one-thousand births or one for every two-hundred fifty births and triplets are about once every *ten-thousand* births. The most common probability for twins in Caucasian women is identical boy babies. After that, identical girls are common and the least likely are fraternal twins, and then one of each. So twins come about once every ninety births in Asian women. Black women birth twins more often, about one set of twins every sixty births, and White and Native American twins occur even more often than that, especially after thirty-five years old. So, time will tell, as they say," Phoebe concluded, taking another bite of pie. Stephen jumped up and, wrapping the handle in a hot pad, grabbed the coffee pot from the stove and served everyone.

"It's decaf, right? I don't need to stay up all night," he explained. Then he asked in a shaky voice, "It doesn't sound too probable we'll have triplets, right?"

"Yes," *Mamm* confirmed. "That's all I make now in the evening —decaf. But don't start worrying about a whole litter, though, okay?" she assured Stephen.

"Mm," Phoebe practically purred as she sipped her creamy coffee. "It's *gut. Denke.*"

Mamm tried to give Phoebe another slice of pie, saying, "Okay, here's some extra calories, missy."

Phoebe said, "I couldn't eat another bite, please, no."

"How much weight do you actually have to gain, then?" *Mamm* wanted to know.

"The latest information says between forty-eight and fifty pounds. They used to tell *mamms* not to gain too much—they said twins should come in tiny packages, but it was all just speculation, really, no proof at all—and it turned out to be counterproductive actually when twins were *kumming* early and were premature. They weren't as developed as they should be," Phoebe quoted from the literature. Remembering her earlier research, she added, "And quadruplets are born in about one in every seven hundred *thousand* pregnancies." Stephen could only shake his head.

Later that evening, Phoebe lay in bed tucked in under their Bear Paws wedding quilt with her hands cradling her still small but growing stomach. Stephen was bathing down in the washroom off the kitchen while Phoebe prayed. The dim kerosene lamp on the dresser, the only light left on in the house sprinkled little shadows around the edges of the room as it flickered. The new polished oak cradle sitting in the corner of the bedroom reflected some of the rays from the lamp. It was slowly filling with little baby items Phoebe had started collecting or *Mamm* had made.

Denke, Gott. *I had no idea You heard me. Please take care of our babies. Please keep them healthy and don't let them* kumm *too early. Denke with all my heart. Give us wisdom as parents and help us to be a prayerful, faithful family. Denke for* Mamm *and* Dat. *Please keep them safe and healthy, too. We're gonna need them here, I'm afraid. Protect our family and show us the way. Amen.*

CHAPTER 2

Phoebe

Monday morning came bright and early. Phoebe realized she was definitely starting to show as she pinned her skirt waist a few inches less to the right than usual. *I hope my dresses have enough room to let out, so we don't have to start sewing all over again,* she thought to herself as she turned toward the mirror on her dresser and positioned her *kapp* in place. *Twins. Who would have thought?* She would be telling the other Four Musketeers the news today at lunch at the nursing school. She went over to her parents' side of the house through the connecting *dawdi haus* door and sat down to breakfast with *Mamm.* Stephen and *Dat* would be along soon, after their morning chores were done, but Phoebe had to be ready when her hired ride arrived. A brown bag lunch was all made and waiting for her at the end of the table. Phoebe sat down as she put two clips into her hairs, securing her *kapp* there.

"I put in some extras," *Mamm* said, noticing Phoebe frowning and eyeing the bag.

"Please don't start giving me tons of sugar. That won't help. We'll work out some snacks and things, okay?" she suggested.

"I still don't believe it. Can you?" *Mamm* asked.

"I know. For sure, it will take some time to get used to. I just want them to be healthy. I'm trying not to think of all the things that could go wrong," she said.

"Welcome to parenthood," her *Mamm* wisely responded. "You're gonna be worrying about them for the next eighteen years or more now. That's what motherhood is all about. It never ends, my dear. They say, 'little people, little problems; big people, big problems.' You'll make a *gut mamm*, though," she added. "And I can't wait to tell the boys."

"Just don't announce it to everyone and their brother just yet, please," Phoebe requested of her *mamm*.

"No, it's just for our family to know. I won't tell anyone else. I promise," *Mamm* said.

"*Denke,*" Phoebe said as she worked on the large bowl of oatmeal her *mamm* had set before her.

"Did you put extra butter and cream in this, *Mamm?*" Phoebe asked.

"*Ya.* Is it okay?"

"Just a bit rich. It's fine. It's *gut,*" she said, continuing to shovel it in by the spoon-full while checking her watch.

Lunch time finally came at the college and The Four Musketeers once again met up at their usual table in the cafeteria. The four Plain girls had been asked by their communities to become LPNs in the hope of having more of a say when members of their community came in contact with the larger medical community. Up until then their Amish, Mennonite and Hutterite settlements had been sorely lacking in good health care. Some unscrupulous doctors had actually taken advantage of the fact that the Plain people didn't carry medical insurance and paid in cash, besides. Having a nurse accompany a mother in labor, for example, might deter or at least make a doctor think twice before insisting on an automatic C-section, thus ensuring him a bigger paycheck. It would also help families care for their dying older people at home when that was their wish. So far, the plan was working beautifully and The Four Musketeers, as they called themselves, were well into their second of the two-year program.

The others began chatting right away with all the latest

happenings at home as they unwrapped their sandwiches. Finally, at a lull in the conversation, Phoebe announced that they went to see their midwife on Saturday morning. The others kept chewing or sipping their drinks until she said quietly, "And we found out it's twins." Everyone froze at that and looked at Phoebe. Hilda asked with her mouth still full, "Is this a joke?"

"No," Phoebe answered, a small smile forming on her lips.

Susanna was the first to speak. "You've got to be kidding me, right?" Phoebe quietly shook her head no. Leah choked on her sandwich and started coughing while Hilda was snorting coffee into her napkin, her eyes fixed on Phoebe.

"Oh... My... G—" Susannah caught herself. "That's incredible. Really? *Really?*"

"We could hear both of them with the Doppler," Phoebe explained. "Loud and clear, too. Like two little ponies racing each other."

Hilda soon recovered and just stared at Phoebe. Finally, she spoke. "Are you excited?"

"Well, *ya.* But we can't have a home birth now. There's more to worry about, I guess. It's all so new." Phoebe took another bite of her mammoth ham and cheese sandwich as the mayonnaise her *mamm* had generously slathered it with, to add to Phoebe's overall calorie intake, dripped out down her chin while she scrambled to find a napkin.

The girls continued to ask questions until the end of lunch time was announced by the automated bell.

"You're all sworn to secrecy now. I mean it. Don't start blabbing, please. Promise?" Phoebe insisted as they headed for the classroom. The others assured her of their silence on the matter.

Phoebe got home that evening just as *Mamm* was putting the finishing touches on supper.

Stephen and *Dat* would still be in the barn for another forty-five minutes or so. Phoebe went into the *dawdi haus* and hung up her shawl and black travelling bonnet, dropping her heavy book bag on a chair. She and Stephen had moved into the little 'grand-parents' apartment' right after their marriage, where they would live until she was done with school. *Mamm* and *Dat* would then switch places with them, giving them the main farmhouse to live in. The advantage to this arrangement was that Phoebe wouldn't have to cook or keep house while she was in school.

She set her shoes on the mat by the door to *Mamm's* kitchen and put on the cozy homemade knitted slippers that *Grossmammi* had just made. Bright pink and purple checks, not exactly Plain, but surprisingly warm.

"So, what's new here?" Phoebe began as she snitched some *shnibbles* from a plate on the counter and began munching. *Mamm* never wasted a thing, taking the doughy offcuts when she made a pie and sprinkled the bits with cinnamon sugar before baking them for a few minutes.

"Well, *ya*, there's some real news today," *Mamm* began. "I was at Miller's shop and they say that, you know that *Englische* midwife called Ruth over in the next district? Well, she had her fifth *bobbel* a few months back. You know the one. Real nice lady. Well, she's been hemorrhaging for a couple of months since and found out she needs a hysterectomy badly, but her baby, Hannah Rose is still nursing and their own parents are pretty unwell or too old to take care of the baby, so she asked Edith and Ezra Miller who have just the one little boy exactly the same age if they will take the baby for a few weeks until Ruth is well. Edith is delighted, so the parents are bringing her up today. I guess the operation is tomorrow in Menomonie. I just hope she doesn't fuss too much or refuse to nurse. We'll see. Edith could always get some formula for the baby, but that would be a lot more work. I can't wait till we have a little one here," *Mamm* added. "Oh. But there's two, isn't there?" she said, still surprised at the revelation.

"*Ya*," Phoebe replied. "That is something. But then if you don't have family nearby, that is a worry. I hope it works out alright. That would be fun, actually."

The same conversation was taking place in many of the houses in the district that night. An *Englische* baby being cared for in an *Amische* family. Unprecedented. Some wondered that the midwife would trust the Amish that much. Others just hoped they wouldn't have an accident while the baby was in their care. What would they do if the baby got sick? Or refused to eat for someone other than her own *mamm?* The way Edith told it to her *mamm* was that Ruth said she didn't trust any of her own friends or neighbors as much as her Amish friends. The fact that Ruth and her family lived a simple life in a log cabin without electricity by choice also puzzled many of the families in the district that night.

"But then some have realized how much of a rat race it is out there in the world and choose to live without TVs or radios and all the other stuff polluting their homes and their *kinner's* minds. Wisconsin is full of what they're calling 'back-to-the-land' folks from what I've read," *Dat* reasoned as he sat down at the table. "There's always been those hippies out there, living in tee pees and yurts and such, but these people are different; serious about what values they want for their kids and willing to do something about it. I give them credit, I really do, homeschooling and all, on their own, no less," he concluded.

"But they don't have the support that we have, surrounded by a whole community who shares and helps them out," Stephen added. "That's got to be mighty hard."

"Pretty daring, if you ask me," Phoebe said. "Then I can see why she'd ask Edith and Ezra. She knows it will be most like their family for the *bobbel.*

Later that evening, Ruth and David and their family pulled up the drive at the Miller's farm in the creaky old station wagon. Ruth carried Hannah Rose bundled up in a quilt as David got the other four out of their car seats and carried a suitcase filled with Hannah's clothes and cloth diapers. Edith took Hannah, and unwrapping her, set her in the playpen in the kitchen next to their sweet little boy, Howard. The two ten-month-olds sat opposite each other, sized each other up for a few moments, and then reached out to start patting each other and laughing.

"Looks like this will work just fine," Edith chuckled.

"We'll sure be praying it all goes well tomorrow," Ezra added.

"Thank you both so much. I can't tell you how much this means to me. I won't have to worry about her at all this way," Ruth said. "Thank you so much," she added, hugging Edith and shaking hands with Ezra.

While the *bobbeli* happily continued to pat and swat at each other, the other children sat quietly at the table in the warm kitchen, slumped in their chairs as if slowly melting. The oldest was seven, then the twins who were five, and then their almost three-year-old little sister, who diligently sucked on her thumb while taking in every detail of the kitchen. It was much like their kitchen in the log cabin, just neater. There were no dirty dishes to be seen. No baskets of clean laundry to fold, no piles of buttons strewn across the table left over from the button strings they were working on earlier that evening. There were no muddy sneakers piled up by the back door, or stray crayons peeking out from under the woodstove. Otherwise, it was familiar enough.

She recognized the strip of yellow fly paper hanging from the ceiling and the mouse-proof gallon jars lined up on a shelf filled with bulk dry goods like rice, beans, oyster crackers, sugar, flour, granola, grape nuts, and split peas. No, not very different from her own cozy home, she surmised.

An old kerosene lantern hung above the table, casting shadows around the little room. A typical Amish kitchen with pegs by the back door for hats and coats, a homemade braided rug by the door with outside footwear lined up behind it, and the wood cook stove with a drying rack suspended above it from the ceiling. Most of the rungs were full of diapers, little t-shirts and muslin and broadcloth dresses. Amish baby boys are often dressed in plain dresses until they are potty-trained, a far easier way to change diapers than wrestling with tiny overalls and pants with snaps and buttons.

The wood stove was still giving off heat though supper was over long ago. A small apartment size gas stove sat in the kitchen off to the side of the wood stove. It was hooked up to a propane canister outside to be used in the hottest weather so the house wouldn't become overheated while cooking on the wood burning larger stove. The wood stove was in operation the rest of the year where the heat it gave off was more than welcomed inside the house. It was the central gathering place, the kitchen was, as blizzards and storms raged outside. A wood stove is an *Amische frau's* pride and joy. The warming oven, a box far above the stove top at the back would be used to set a bowl of rising bread dough covered with a cloth or glass jars of fermenting yogurt. A small stone-ware crockery jar might also be up there, containing sourdough starter happily bubbling away, set far apart from any drafty corners around the rest of the room.

The wood stove's main cooking area on the stovetop held four 'burners'—round cast-iron plates that could be removed by inserting a metal handle into a slot and lifting up, setting it aside to give a pot or a pan direct heat from the firebox below. A wood box would be on the floor next to the stove, which one of the children would be tasked with keeping full of short logs and kindling. In the coldest months, the fire there would be banked and stuffed with wood before bedtime and still provide coals in the morning in time to stoke it up again to start cooking breakfast. The right side of the stovetop would cover the large built-in oven for baking, with several racks inside. Some stoves also have a water reservoir, taking advantage of the fire to have access to hot water all day. A jar of black, waxy Stove Polish Paste keeps wood stoves shining bright. It is applied when the stove is cold and the ashes have been removed. It bakes itself on when the fire is again lit, producing a beautiful finish that shines and prevents rust spots.

"Oh, I almost forgot," Edith said, hurrying to the sideboard in the kitchen, and bringing back a platter of fresh, giant sugar cookies. "Help yourselves," she said to the children who suddenly revived, sitting up and obediently pounced on the cookies.

"I don't know how you have time to bake." Ruth laughed. "I barely get the wash and the dishes done each day."

Edith served everyone cambric tea while the children devoured the monster cookies. She broke two chunks off of one and handed them to the babies in the play pen who immediately stuffed them into their mouths, quickly forgetting their game.

Finally, David spoke. "Well, we better get back before it's too late. We really can't thank you two enough."

Then Ezra asked, "Who's gonna help you with these other *kinner?*"

"I guess it's just me," David replied. "Ruth's done the shopping and planned out some simple meals and she'll be home in a couple of days and then recovering for about three weeks, and I took some time off teaching so it shouldn't be too bad," he said, though sounding rather unconvinced himself as he wrestled into his denim jacket.

"It's got to be hard without your families nearby," Ezra commented.

"It is, but we've managed so far," Ruth added optimistically, though she felt herself entering shaky ground here as the time to leave without her precious baby was nearing. She took a few deep breaths as she stood to gather up her other little ones.

"Come on, you lot," David said as he helped each of the children into their jackets or sweaters that had found their way to the floor while they visited. "Say goodbye to Hannah Rose," he said. "Tell her we'll see her soon."

"Can't I stay with her?" little Rachel mournfully pleaded.

"No. They'll have enough work with two," her dad said, ushering her out the door.

The children had been informed of the plan ahead of time, and cheerfully said goodbye to Hannah Rose who ignored them as she resumed her game with Howard.

Ruth snuck out the door among the children as she felt hot tears begin to cascade down her cheeks. She quickly recovered, wiping her eyes and blowing her nose as they buckled the children into their seats. Taking her place in the front seat of the car, she finally turned around and addressed the children.

"How were those cookies, huh?"

"They were giant! How come you never buy us M&Ms?" Avi asked.

"Yummy," little Rachel agreed.

"You don't need more sugar," their mother replied. "You'll probably all be up half the night as it is," she lamented. Turning back as her husband started the car, she found herself silently weeping into her handkerchief as she began to imagine everything that could possibly go wrong, both with the surgery and with little Hannah Rose. Will she miss her *mamm?* Will she somehow be scarred by the interruption in maternal-infant bonding? What had they done? Did they have any better option though, really?

A little over an hour and a half later, the old station wagon lumbered its way off the rural route, and onto the shoulder next to the driveway. The rest of it had been washed out during the last rainstorm, so they still had to walk the last quarter mile up to the log cabin. Amidst their complaining, Ruth said finally, "You know guys, Edith gave me a bag of those cookies to bring home and whoever doesn't whine tonight gets one in the morning."

The grumbling stopped instantly at that, and the little horde ran the rest of the way up the long hill in the semi-darkness as fast as their little legs would take them. They piled into the kitchen finally as their dad lit the kerosene lamps and took turns brushing their teeth at the sink. Then they obediently went up to the loft, taking turns on the commode in the alcove, and changed into pajamas or nightgowns before wiggling into their beds. David turned all the lamps out but one in the kitchen and carefully brought it up to the bedroom loft where they all slept on two futons, setting it on a high shelf. He and Ruth prepared for bed and snuggled in to hear the latest episode of *Little House on the Prairie* as he read to them. One by one the little ones fell asleep, little Rachel the first to drop off with the perpetual thumb in her mouth. They would have to find a way to address that habit before it affected her teeth. Then Ruth got up and blew out the waning wick.

CHAPTER 3

Ivan

Hilda grabbed her purse and school bag filled with books out of the car and waved Leah goodbye. "You have a good evening!" she yelled. "Don't study too hard." As Leah pulled the car back out of the driveway, Hilda checked the mailbox before hiking up to the house. The first letter there was addressed to her. She ran the rest of the way and threw down her bags as soon as she got in the house, ripping open the envelope.

November 25th

Dear Hilda,

I can't stop thinking about you. It is really an answer to prayer meeting you. I am older than you at thirty, but I just never got into dating much. I'd go to some of the singings and work pushes where all the young chaps and girls put in an extra couple of hours after supper in the factory to catch up on the biggest orders that week, and then had snack together before going home, and got along with everyone just fine but was starting to wonder if I'd be a bachelor forever. So I'd been praying, asking what God has in mind for my life. I thought maybe work in the missions; there's never enough people for that. And then I met you.

I can't wait till you can visit here. It's quite different from your community. Some things, at least. There's a whole lot more of the old Swiss influence still felt here that the Grabills brought over in the 1780s.

Some things are more conservative here than other Mennonite churches. The Wisler Mennonites still hang on to some of the original things like not having cars or telephones, but that is dying out slowly.

One thing that is still going strong is our yodeling. I know that'll probably come as a surprise, but it's true. Some say that the cows like it. That's why they give so much milk. We get top dollar for the highest butterfat content in the county, but then our breed is known for that. Either way, you can hear yodeling every morning wherever you go. It's quite fun. We get up young people yodeling contests and gatherings sometimes.

Other things have changed though that not all agree on, like how some interpret dress, what modern technology to accept or refuse to use, and things like Sunday school and prayer meetings. So, the result is that different groups use the church hall at different times, whatever flavor worship they espouse.

My family is so happy I finally found someone. Mom is over the moon. I told them we're just getting to know each other, but you know how parents are. I think I told you we are six children. I am the eldest, with three boys and three girls. I have one younger brother and one younger sister, both married and each has one baby already. I hope you can get away for a long weekend, maybe during Christmas. The Greyhound is the easiest way to get here, and you can do it overnight. We can also check ahead with the Mennonite Your Way Directory and see who's travelling those dates. That's free, though most offer to help out with the gas. You can register ahead of time and then tell them where you want to go. I'll look on this end, too. There's always The Budget, also. Check out the classifieds where people post van trips, and such.

I can't close this letter without telling you about one of the most extraordinary books I just finished reading: Neither Wolf Nor Dog. I truly believe no one should go away on mission without reading it first. I honestly did not think I was prejudiced in any way, until I read it. This Native elder tells his story and tells us what is wrong with his Native People, what is wrong with us White People and what is wrong about the way we've all been trying to get along and honor each other. I was blown away. I was forced to reexamine everything I thought was true about mission. You must find time to read it, my love.

Well, it's late. I am thinking of you always with much love and prayers,

Yours,

Ivan Grabill

November 27th

Dear Ivan,

Your letter brought me much joy. I miss you already. I am still laughing about yodeling to the cows when you're milking them. I've gotta see that! Do your cows yodel back, or do they moo like normal cows?

I wish I had time to read. That book sounds so intriguing. School is all I've time for, and even then, I am burning the candle at both ends, getting up early to review before tests and staying up late writing papers or reading yet another textbook. I can't imagine having time to enjoy a book again. Really!

We're preparing for Christmas here. All the school children are buzzing with this year's Christmas play. It is always the highlight of the season for the families.

It's back to school here for me. We've got a mammoth paper to write and then studying for our finals. Both are due just after Christmas, but it will be here before we know it. We have some time off after New Years. I've already checked in with the 'Mennonite Your Way' people. I just have to call them when we have some dates for visiting. My folks are actually a host family for them. We've hosted folks over the years when they come this way and needed a place to stay. It is always interesting visiting with new people. We keep the guest room ready all year 'round. When there's the big teachers' conference here each year we get guests, and not just Plain people. We get to screen them a bit before they come, but we've never had to refuse anyone. Now I take that back. One time a group of bikers were biking across the U.S. and asked to stay. There were about twenty-five of them and they wanted to all double up, you know, boyfriends with girlfriends and we said that our church families could house them but in separate bedrooms, and they didn't want to do that. A few stayed with us, but the rest went to a nearby campground and *pitched tents. The girls that stayed with us gave us a whole lecture at breakfast about why we shouldn't be buying bananas ever—at all—and all the boycotts that are going on to support the growers back wherever they grow bananas. We listened but they wouldn't eat the bananas we had put out with oatmeal that breakfast. If I remember right, their whole trip across America was to inform people about the bananas. I think I would try to find bigger causes than bananas to champion. Maybe the Kingdom of Heaven? Want to bike across America with me? That would be a blast, huh? Maybe with some other young couples? Gosh, I love that idea!*

Time for bed. Have to be up early for school tomorrow.

With love and prayers always,
   Hilda

P. S. Don't buy bananas from South America if you can avoid it.

CHAPTER 4
The Four Musketeers

A
s The Four Musketeers dashed to the cafeteria, Susanna called down the hall to the others, "Have I got a story for you!" When they were all assembled with their drinks and brown bag lunches, she began.

"Last Friday night when I got home, the whole *'hof* was buzzing about the accident that happened in the kitchen around noon. It was absolutely horrible! How they told it to me is that the cook, Liz, was just finished making French fries and got one of the other girls to help her lift the oil tray out of the fryer and set it on the floor on newspaper to cool off. She wanted to clean the stove top before they heard the noon lunch bell.

"Now she had her oldest niece, Becky, who is ten, watching the little ones for her kitchen week, but one got away from the babysitter and ran to see her *mudder* in the kitchen. Ida is two. Just as she got into the kitchen, Becky ran after her and called her back. Ida somehow turned around when she heard Becky yell for her and tripped and fell backwards into the hot oil." At this point, the others could only gasp at what this implied.

"Everyone panicked, and the *basels* got her into a sink full of cold water and called an ambulance. They took her to the burn unit in St. Paul, where they stabilized her. She'll be there for months."

"They should have older *kinner* babysitting," Phoebe scolded, shaking her head.

"There's more accidents than there should be in Plain communities," Leah lamented.

Then Hilda spoke. "I'm afraid there isn't the education about safety that there should be, and the public health department can only do so much."

Then Phoebe told Susanna to go on.

"Well, last night, it was Sunday, right? I went with a van to the hospital. Ida was alert and didn't seem to be in much pain, though they are giving her mega-meds for that, I imagine. It was amazing, but her neck, face and hands weren't burned at all. They had the rest of her wound up like a mummy in bandages and she was resting on a crib-size waterbed. Her chances look good, though over ninety percent of her body was burned."

"How are her parents doing?" Hilda wanted to know.

"Well," Susanna continued. "They weren't there when we got to the hospital though they'd been there the whole time so far. The nurse said they were staying in a motel down the street. So we went there after we visited with the *dindla*. We found the motel alright. They had a teeny tiny room and they told us their steward from home had come down after them and arranged everything so nicely, bringing them food in a big cooler and some clothes and gave them enough money to cover for a while. The *vetters* from the '*hof*—the men—go down to the city pretty often on business so they assured Sam and Liz they'd be bringing down supplies for the room every week and keep them stocked up. It's over a four-hour drive one way.

"When we got there, they had the TV on and were watching something called *Archie Bunker* and were laughing hysterically. It was really funny. This old guy is a complete bigot and makes all these bizarre statements, and his wife, Edith, is something of a space cookie and doesn't get the jokes and stuff at all. She is just a hoot! You know, they'd never even seen a TV before."

"Anyway, I'm glad they got permission to watch the TV. It will give them a break from all the drama at the hospital. They can clean up there and sleep and make some simple meals and still walk down to the hospital every day. Everyone back at the *'hof* are watching their other kids at home. Liz had just had Daniel a couple of months ago, too. They miss them terribly, but Ida needs them just now. I was thinking we could all go down there one day. Visit Ida and get to see the burn unit, bring the parents some treats. Yeah, we could take them out somewhere for lunch, even. That's gotta be hard, hanging out so far from home, worrying about their little one," Susanna concluded.

"You never know what'll happen next with kids, do you?" Phoebe asked. "You can only pray and hope every day that you don't get something like that happening. Your whole life can change in a flash just like that, *eh?* You really do end up worrying about them for the next eighteen years, for sure."

She continued, "It must have been some kind of bad-luck accident weekend or something. We had a bit of it on Saturday evening. The next farm over from us, the Yoders, have seven kids and their *mamm* had sent them out to play before supper to 'get out all the beans' before they came back in. Well, they decided to play sardines—you know where the first one goes out and the others close their eyes and count to twenty and then the others go out one by one and when they find the first one, they hide out with him, all squishing in like sardines in a tin, until the very last one finds them.

"Well, Max hid first, and it took forever for the next one to find him, but he finally did and all the others did, too, one by one. Their *mamm* was about to call them in for supper when she heard this horrible ruckus, screaming and all. Turns out Max had dragged a ladder out from the barn and propped it up on the back side of the outhouse and climbed up there. He lay down flat on the tilting tar paper and shingled roof until the next one finally found him when he came out the back of the barn. By the time the last girl found them and climbed up, they'd all squeezed over and Max fell off the roof, breaking his arm. *Gut* thing that's all he broke. Their *dat* got the neighbor to drive them to the clinic, which was still open. They didn't eat supper till close to ten that night!"

CHAPTER 5
Ivan & Hilda

At last, school let out for the holidays and Ivan couldn't wait for Hilda to arrive. The next morning, she hastily packed her rucksack and went downstairs. The children were still asleep, but her parents were up at 4:00 a.m. to see her off. Her mother had packed two brown bags with breakfast and lunch sandwiches. Each bag even had a small label indicating which meal it was meant for.

"You must have been up by three," Hilda said. "You didn't have to, Ma."

"I wanted to, honey. I am so excited for you. Now you have a wonderful time. I can't wait to have you back and hear all about it," her mother said as she hugged Hilda. Just then, they heard the van crunch on the gravel driveway. Hilda quickly hugged her dad and mom, grabbed the two brown bags and slung the rucksack onto her shoulder before running out of the house.

The van was full; every seat but one taken. Suitcases and knapsacks were tucked into every remaining nook and cranny as were Tupperware containers of bars, cookies and snack mix.

"Thank you so much for fitting me in," Hilda began as she settled into the last available seat and balanced the two brown bags on her lap. Her rucksack was sitting on her feet in front of her.

"Who are you going to see in Indiana?" a girl named Laura,

about Hilda's age asked.

"My boyfriend, Ivan Grabill, is near Goshen," she replied.

A woman sitting in the last seat in the back piped up, "Oh! I know his father. Nicest family."

"It's a small world," a man in the front passenger seat added. "He's my cousin. How about that?"

"Do you have a wedding date yet, dear?" an older woman sitting next to Hilda asked.

"We're still getting to know each other," Hilda explained. "This is my first trip to meet his family."

"That should be such fun," the older woman exclaimed. "Walter is my husband. He's driving up there. We've been married forty-nine years. Where does the time go?"

"I can't imagine," Hilda commented then. *What is that even like?* Hilda wondered to herself. *Are they still in love? Do they just take it all for granted by then? Do they still, uh, you know...* she pondered, then quickly attempted to erase that last thought as she surveyed the jolly, plump woman next to her.

They continued to chat for the next hour. Some got out books to read in the car. The older woman finally found her knitting bag after she'd enlisted all the others to hunt for it. It had been shoved under her seat. Others in the van napped. Around noon, Walter pulled the van into a rest stop along the freeway. Everyone got out and stretched their stiff limbs before gingerly walking to the facilities. After hastily eating their sandwiches and grabbing a few of the treats in the Tupperware containers, they were off again as the Chex Mix and the sweets made the rounds a second time.

Around 5:00 p.m. they stopped once again, this time at a Perkins restaurant just off the highway.

"How much farther?" the other girl in the van asked once they were settled at a large round table.

Walter answered. "About three more hours I figure, until we drop the first bunch off near Chicago. Then two and a half to Goshen. We'll stay there the night after dropping the rest of you off and me and the Mrs. will get to Maumee, Ohio by lunch time. We'll switch drivers after supper here."

They all gave their orders to the waitress then, Walter letting her know they wanted to get back on the road sooner than later. She promised to pass that along to the kitchen.

Back in the van, the plump wife then asked Hilda, "What book were you reading earlier, dear? It looks pretty, uh, academic?"

"I'm in nursing school. I'll graduate in June. The community asked me to go to college and get my LPN in order to help out more at home with our moms and the older people," she explained.

"Why, that is a brilliant idea," she replied. "Walter, did you hear that?" she called to the front seat. "Why don't we do that back home? A simply marvelous idea. I love it! Yes, I will talk to the bishop about that. Lovely idea, for sure," she said, nodding to herself while patting Hilda's knee next to her.

There were plenty of questions from the other passengers. The time went quickly, and they were soon in the outskirts of Chicago as announced by the driver who had pulled up to a large house. They all piled out when Laura's father came out and encouraged them to all come in 'just for a second' and stretch. Laura's mother had pie and coffee ready for the travelers. Laura had brought along two of her friends who would also be staying with her family.

"Oh, you didn't have to do all this," the plump woman from the van said upon her return from the bathroom while eagerly eyeing the pies on the table.

"You can just eat and run, please, just to keep you all going," Laura's mother said, which is exactly what they did. The pumpkin and cherry pies were still warm from the oven as they sat down, melting the vanilla ice cream she had put on top of each generous slice.

Walter thanked the family for the snack and Laura's family thanked him for delivering their daughter and her friends safely to them.

Soon they were back on the road, full of pie and rejuvenated by the coffee.

Walter announced that Goshen would be their next stop, where they would be dropping Hilda and the last of the other passengers off. Then he and his wife would be staying overnight before making their way to their families in Ohio.

"A cousin of mine owns a bed-and-breakfast there," he explained, "just outside of Goshen on their farm and insisted we spend the night there catching up with them. We'll stay just tonight and sleep in a bit before driving to Ohio tomorrow. I haven't seen them in quite a while," Walter elaborated.

"They're known all over for their breakfasts," his wife added, licking her lips.

"The tourist catalogues call it 'gourmet breakfasts,'" she continued, emphasizing the fact by her raised eyebrows.

Walter had arranged for all those leaving them in Goshen to be picked up at a certain restaurant right off the highway. As the van pulled into the parking lot, Hilda could see Ivan already out of his car and waiting with his hands in his pockets. He ran right up to the door of the vehicle and helped the passengers out one at a time. Hilda was the last one out. Taking both her hands, he practically lifted her out of the van and into a huge hug.

"You can put me down now," Hilda protested, laughing. "I missed you too."

"You have no idea," Ivan said while still hugging her, afraid to end the thrilling moment. "I've been counting the minutes here," he said as he gave her a final squeeze and set her down on her feet finally.

"That was a looonnnnggggg ride," she said, stretching her arms and rolling her shoulders. "I never thought we'd get here." She waved the others goodbye and ran over to thank Walter and his wife who took Hilda's hand and leaning into her whispered coyly, "He is cute, isn't he?"

Holding hands again, she and Ivan headed for his car. He threw her bag into the back seat and opened her door.

"You might have to let go of me to get into the other seat," she teased him.

"This is my little sister, Edna," he said, nodding toward the back seat. "She wanted to come along for the ride," Ivan explained when they were all seated.

Finally, they were on the road, holding hands once again.

"How far to your house?" she asked.

"About forty-five minutes," he replied. "They are all so excited to meet you. Only four of us are still at home. My brother Klaus and sister Agnes are married. They might come over tomorrow. They live in the area. Then there's Menno, Edna here, and Helena still at home."

As he talked, Hilda watched his face animatedly describing each one. His sandy hair had been ruffled by the wind in the parking lot and still stood straight up in places. The auburn high-lights were still visible in spite of the total disarray above. He was well tanned. Obviously, he'd been working outside all summer and though suntan fades once the summer is over, he still retained much of the golden glow the season had bestowed on him, the blond hairs on his hands attesting to that fact. He certainly was tall. His head almost brushed the top of the car as he drove. His knees definitely touched the steering wheel, she noticed as she thought about the flannel shirt she had made him for his Christmas gift, glad she'd chosen an extra-large/tall pattern. The blue plaid would be perfect on him and match his washed denim jeans. She'd never seen him in anything else.

"Mennonite territory," she stated simply as the mailbox signs suddenly started to appear.

"Absolutely," he agreed. "We're almost there," he said as they passed the first sign, which he read out loud. WITH CHRIST, LIFE IS WORTH LIVING... READ ROMANS 6. Soon they were at the house. "Did I tell you, we can now order the mailbox signs online? A set of twelve, one for each month. Someone is cashing in on a good thing," he laughed.

"Oh good. You're here," his mother said as they walked into the house on her way to greet Hilda. "We didn't know if your ride would be on time."

"We made really good time," Hilda replied. "It's so good to finally meet you!"

"And you, too," Ivan's father said as he shook her hand.

"My folks send their greetings too," Hilda added.

"We'll look forward to meeting them sometime soon," Ivan's mother said. "I have dessert ready if you'd like. When you called, you said that you stopped for supper on the way."

"Oh, this is perfect, thank you," Hilda agreed, surveying the table. When everyone was sitting down, Ivan began the introductions.

"You met Mom and Dad," he began as his mother passed China dessert plates with huge slices of cake down the long table while one of the girls poured coffee.

"Please call us Cornelius and Kathy," his mother hurried to add. Then she said, "This is Menno, and across from him is Edna whom you've met already, and Helena has the coffee pot." They all nodded their greetings, smiling.

Menno spoke up first. "We've heard all about you since Ivan returned...that's *all* we've heard about. But don't worry, it's all good."

Edna scowled at him as Helena added, "Sounds like you two were made for each other."

"That's what I'd like to think," Hilda bravely ventured, blushing involuntarily once again.

"And you are a nurse, I mean almost," Cornelius said.

"It will become official I hope, in June," Hilda explained, "if I pass my finals. I'm praying and studying hard."

"I really think that is great. We should consider that here, don't you think, Kathy?" he added.

"Maybe. Pretty radical, you know progressive. Might be hard to convince folks here, I'd guess. Do you get along with the other students? Is it hard?" Kathy wanted to know.

"There are four of us Plain girls. It is actually great fun. The others are used to us now and I haven't had any problems. Two of the regular students even made long skirts to match ours. We thought that was pretty keen. And I've learned so much," Hilda said. "I will be glad when it's done, though, I have to admit. Two years is a long time. It's all I do: study, go to school, study some more, sleep and eat. I don't think I can cram anymore into my brain at this point. I'm so ready to be done, for sure."

They continued to visit as they enjoyed the dessert. Then Ivan suggested he and Hilda go for a walk. It was already dusk, but they hadn't had time to talk alone.

Ivan held the door for her as Hilda walked outside. She already had butterflies banging the inside walls of her stomach. Taking a slow breath, she turned to him as soon as the door to the house closed.

"Finally," Ivan whispered. "I can't believe you're here."

"I know," Hilda said.

"Can I hug you?" he ventured.

She answered by leaning into his chest and wrapping her arms around his waist. He was too tall for her to reach any higher. He gave her a strong hug back. Neither one wanted this moment to ever end.

"Oh, I've missed you," Ivan began. Then, taking her hand, they walked down the long driveway and onto the county road. There were no cars to be seen. The quiet night was only punctuated by a dog barking and a cow mooing from some nearby barn. Every star appeared to be out, and the moon was already casting shadows on the trees and farmhouses. They were quiet then as they walked along the road. They passed a mailbox sign that read, READ THE BIBLE. IT IS GOD SPEAKING... READ ROMANS 10:17.

Then Hilda spoke. "I really want our relationship to be centered on prayer. I think God brought us together and I can't think of any other way to move forward. Do you feel that way?"

"Yes. I have been thinking about it a lot. I look at our parents who are still in love, still living a committed life. That is special. It is really blessed. They have their priorities straight. Then I look at some of the young people in the world and in our church, too, who are infatuated with the idea of love. Who are living a superficial life, nothing deep to live for. Maybe it comes with age, but I want our lives to count for something. For His kingdom. I think we are being called to do that together, to help one another to do that."

"It feels like a huge responsibility. Like we are being asked to take on a huge task. But together, we are stronger than on our own. And if we can pray together every day and keep that as our focus, hopefully we can't go wrong, don't you think?" Hilda asked, stopping and turning toward him.

Ivan bent down at that point and gently kissed Hilda's cheek.

"You are right," he said. "I think we will both be given grace, and wisdom and insight. In a way, it also feels like a battle, a spiritual battle, to stay alert and renounce the world of pride and worldly success and stay on the humble path. I think our parents must have instilled this in us. Hopefully we can do the same for our children," he said as he once more took her hand, and they continued walking.

It was late when they returned to the house. The guest room was ready for which Hilda was deeply grateful as she changed into her flannel nightgown and slid between the crisp sheets that smelled like the country: crops, animals, wildflowers, and all. An abbreviated though heartfelt prayer of thanks went up as she surrendered to sleep, wondering what the next day might bring.

Edith awoke with an uncertain feeling. Was it foreboding? The bedroom was quiet. Too quiet. She flipped back the quilt to sit up and look at the cribs against the wall. They were empty, though after day one they'd let the 'twins' sleep together, which they themselves had insisted on. Ezra wasn't in bed, either. She jumped up and, without even putting on her slippers, ran to the kitchen across the chilly linoleum. She took in the scene there and breathed out a long sigh of relief.

"I don't believe you!" she almost laughed. "Why didn't you wake me?"

"Well, when I got back from doing the chores these two thieves were up, playing quietly, so I got them in the playpen and started breakfast." Edith surveyed the floor of the playpen. Ezra had given the *bobbeli* quite an odd assortment of whatever was at hand in the kitchen, his attempt at entertaining them while he bravely began making breakfast. There were hot pads, wooden spoons, a ball of yarn, a ladle, and a set of plastic measuring cups.

CHAPTER 6
Ezra & Edith

"Lord knows you've hardly gotten enough sleep lately while running after Hunky and Dory here all day long and some nights, too. They're quite happy. I think two is actually easier than just one. You don't have to play with them as much—ya know, entertain them—since they are so happy with their ready-made playmate. I don't know what we're going to do when she has to go home. Howard will be devastated," Ezra predicted.

"I know *I'll* be devastated. Hannah Rose is such a joy. I love her already. Well, best get them changed and dressed. We'll have to leave for church-Sunday in less than an hour. *Denke* for letting me sleep in," Edith said. "Let's dress them the same again."

"She's not a little dolly," Ezra said, chuckling. "I'll go get dressed. Corn meal mush is almost ready here."

After church, which was held at the Lehman's farm this time, the meal was being set up outside. It was unusually warm for the first week in April, but the *mamms* were grateful they were able to sit outside with their children and didn't have to keep tabs on them inside the house. That always made the parents nervous, hoping they weren't getting into something they shouldn't or breaking something that wasn't theirs. The *kinner* would often run riot after being forced to sit still on the benches during the two or sometimes three-hour service. Whole herds of free-range little people would stampede through the house, though out in someone's yard was definitely preferable. The fact that 'church cookies'—those heavy butter or lard-laden sugar cookies—and pretzels or little handheld *shnitz* pies were passed out halfway through the ordeal didn't hold their attention for long once they were consumed.

Edith shook out the big blanket she had retrieved from the buggy while Ezra stood with a toddler under each arm. When she had it spread out on the grass, he plunked them down, facing each other. They began whatever game had been interrupted when church ended with the last slow hymn and were both soon chortling and playfully swatting at each other.

They were dressed identically. Howard's little bowl haircut designated him as a boy, even though he still wore a baby dress, a generic smock that made it easier to change babies than trousers with buttons or snaps. As soon as he was potty-trained, he'd graduate into little boy clothes, identical tiny copies of his *dat's*.

"Edith!" the girl fairly shouted, turning a few heads that were close enough to be startled.

Edith looked up from distributing dry Cheerios to the *bobbeli* from a Ziploc bag in her *kavli*.

"You didn't know we had *ztzvilling?*" Edith stated. The same scenario was repeated close to a dozen times that day, much to Edith's delight. The fact was that she had fallen in love with the baby, with nursing her to sleep every night and caring for her along with their own *bobbel*. They were the same age, almost a year old. They both ate voraciously and only nursed for comfort before bed in the evenings. Edith knew from the beginning that by taking Hannah Rose, they were just helping the midwife Ruth out for a few weeks after she had emergency surgery. But the fact was she had grown fond of the darling, precious child and loved her as her own.

Ezra finally appeared with two plates piled high with food and sat down on the blanket, careful not to spill any of the good Sunday fare. The two inquisitive *bobbeli* each rolled over from a sitting position in order to crawl at breakneck speed toward the food. The blanket definitely hampered their attempts at crawling, landing them flat on their faces, despite their stiff-legged crab walk to avoid catching the skirt of their dresses, but the determined little rug rats forged on until they were in front of Edith and Ezra, mouths open, pudgy little hands grabbing the closest morsels.

"Do net!" Ezra said firmly. Both little hands instantly retreated.

"Sits ana," he ordered, not unkindly. Like two little trained seals, they complied.

"Patties down?" he asked after a moment, to which they both laid their hands in their laps. When he lowered his head and closed his eyes, they followed suit. After another moment, he looked up to see both little rascals still squeezing their eyes tight shut. He cleared his throat and the two little pairs of eyes popped open, though the hands stayed in their laps.

"Gut," he praised them.

"We've got them pretty well taught, eh?" Edith commented with a smile.

"If you don't do it when they're little, you might as well give up," Ezra agreed, "and then you'll have totally out-of-control *kinner* before they're even teenagers."

Edith put their bibs on and took two little Peter Rabbit plastic bowls out of the diaper bag. She buttered a slice of bread, then cut it into little cubes and put them into the bowls. She put in two little spoons also, though she knew they wouldn't use them, but that lesson would be taught in the days ahead.

She proceeded to put chunks of potato from the potato salad on her own plate into the two bowls along with other choice morsels. When the family had finished eating, Ezra produced an assortment of cookies from the napkin he had hidden under a corner of the blanket when he returned from the food tables earlier. Giving each *bobbeli* a cookie, he heard a faint word spoken from each one that he took to be a *'denke'* in baby talk. Hannah Rose was still holding a spoon in her left hand and taking the cookie with her right hand after thoroughly examining it, proceeded to eat it.

Ezra repeated his own *"Denke,"* just to reinforce the habit.

Edith got up and headed for the dessert table where the

coffee urn was sitting and brought back two steaming mugs. She knew the babies would be occupied with their cookies long enough for them to enjoy their coffee. Producing a water bottle from the diaper bag she half-filled two sippy cups which she gave to the two.

People continued to walk by the picnic blanket on their way to the tables or the outhouse, occasionally doing a double take to which Edith again repeated the ruse that she'd had twins. She enjoyed it especially when one of the passersby asked, "Are they identical?" The first time that happened when the baby had first come to them, she patiently explained how they couldn't be identical if one was a boy and one was a girl, but more recently she saved herself the trouble of the long explanation about fraternal twins and simply agreed by saying, "Uh huh" and nodded sweetly. She told Ezra they'd eventually figure it out on their own. Or not.

The fact was, however, that she dreaded the day that was fast approaching when Hannah Rose's family would return to claim her. Ezra had warned her all along not to get too attached, but how could her motherly heart *not* bond with the beautiful little *Englische* girl?

That day did indeed come, and all too quickly. Hannah's mother had written a letter only last week that she was slowly recovering from the surgery and planned to come up the next weekend to get her.

On Monday, two days after the letter had come, Edith carefully washed all of Hannah Rose's clothes and diapers and packed them into the suitcase her family had brought them in. She examined one little plum-colored dress with its matching pinafore, thinking to herself how similar it was to their own *Amische* dresses, but then she remembered that Ruth had made most of the family's clothes after she'd mastered the old treadle sewing machine she'd found at a barn sale. *They sure are determined to live simply without electricity, but how long can they hold out without a church community surrounding them to support such a lifestyle? All on their own. Plus home schooling. That must be lonely. But with five* kinner *I guess you aren't all that lonely*, Edith mused to herself. *Or plain too busy to think...*

CHAPTER 7

Noah & Faith

N oah gave his wife a quick kiss goodbye as he ushered the two little girls outside. It was a beautiful crisp autumn day. He noted all the leaves rushing into the mudroom as they closed the door and headed to the barn. *Have to rake up the leaves later today,* he thought to himself.

It was a *Samschdaag.* His wife, Faith, had handed him a grocery list after breakfast. He would take the buggy to town and have the errands done in plenty of time to get back to the farm before dinner time. The two little girls were excited to have 'daddy time.' Faith checked their blue pinafores for any spilled food after breakfast as she adjusted their stiff going-out black bonnets, tiny replicas of her own. Buttoning up their small black sweaters, and tying the laces on their navy canvas sneakers, she declared them passable for a trip to town.

Hope would be turning five next week, and Charity was almost four. The *bobbel* of the family, Patience, was only two months old. Faith wasn't keen to take her out quite yet. Too many colds and flus out there, and the *Englische* visitors who were always roaming around town especially on weekends, always wanting to take pictures of the children, often not even procuring permission first, just snapping away with their cameras. She preferred to stay home. The baby would be napping soon, and she could get some of the housework done with the older ones out from under her feet. They were good little helpers, though. They were happiest when she gave them each a dusting rag and they followed her around the house dusting everything they came across: the spindles on *Dat's* rocker, the windowsills, the lid of the toy chest, the cupboard doors and then even their dollies. They knew some day they would have their own families and farms to care for and they would know just how to keep them clean and tidy.

The horse properly *redded* up to the buggy, Noah walked her out of the forebay of the barn and into the dazzling sunlight outside. He pulled himself up and sat on the bench, checking that the little girls were sitting behind him on the padded seat that was secured to the floorboards, no little hands sticking out the windows. Bracing his feet against the footrest at the dashboard, he had not gone more than a few yards down the drive when both girls squealed and at the same time pointed to the big maple tree by the road.

"Es gschwall!" they both shouted, bouncing up and down on the bench. Noah looked in the direction of the tree and saw a whole family of squirrels romping and chasing one another on the ground and racing up through the branches.

"Ya, es gschwall" for sure," he agreed. The two wouldn't be starting school and learning English until the following fall. The Dutch twins were barely a year apart. There would have been another baby after Charity, but a late miscarriage dashed that hope. But now they had Patience.

Noah and Faith felt blessed, nonetheless. The farm was producing well. Calves were still coming all that fall, expanding their own herd with extra ones selling at the auction each week as fast as they were born. The garden was still overflowing with vegetables, faster than Faith could can it all in jars. The *kinner* were healthy, and their marriage remained strong. Their families lived nearby, and their church district provided support and spiritual nourishment throughout the year. What more could a person wish for?

Half an hour later, Noah tied up the buggy to the hitching rail outside of Miller's Mercantile. He lifted each of his daughters out of the buggy, setting them by his side until he could grab a hand in each of his and go into the store, but not before he stopped and squatted down next to them reminding them that they could each earn a peppermint stick if they didn't touch anything and stayed right by him in the store the whole time. They both nodded solemnly, already practically tasting that rarest of treats.

That errand done, Noah brought the mare onto the shoulder of the main road and drove another twenty minutes south to the shopping center. He repeated the drill, getting the girls out of the buggy, then grabbing the two now sticky hands and reminding them to *beheef dich* when they went in. While each continued sucking on a peppermint stick, they silently nodded that they understood.

Directing the shopping cart, he went up and down the aisles with the two little girls holding each other's hand and trailing behind, getting everything on the list Faith had given him. Peanut butter was the last item which he placed in the wagon and headed to the checkout counter. One more stop before they could head home.

The drill was once more carried out this time in reverse, and they left the store with girls and groceries lined up in the back of the buggy. The health food co-op was the last stop. Once again, holding two very sticky hands, they entered the store. Finding the family-friendly restroom, Noah removed a clean bandana handkerchief from the inside pocket of his going-to-town jacket, wiped the two little noses and then cleaned first his hands and then the girls', vigorously rubbing their chins with a wet paper towel until the pink goo was gone. Potty stops were in order before the trip home. Then, checking them one last time, he proceeded to get the last things on the list: honey, nutritional yeast flakes, Mother's Milk Organic Herbal Tea, Dr. Donsbach's prenatal vitamins and lanolin cream. Choosing three small apples on his way to the checkout lane, he waited while the family ahead of them finished up.

Noah was barely out the door when a camera caught him off guard before he could lower the rim of his straw hat or turn away.

The lady tourist squealed with delight, commenting to Noah how absolutely angelic his adorable little girls were.

Barely grunting in agreement, he hustled the two over to the buggy and deposited them and the bag of groceries inside. Hauling himself up and sitting squarely on the front bench seat, he slapped the horse's rump with the reins harder than was necessary and called *"Gay."* The horse was soon clip-clopping along the gravel shoulder of the two-lane road heading north.

The road out of town slowly passed the stores. The farm store, the John Deere tractor outlet, the Five & Dime, the pharmacy, the little Dew Drop Inn café that the locals frequented, and then the truck stop. Up ahead, Noah glanced at the row of grain elevators and feed mill warehouses. He wiggled out of his jacket, tossing it into the back of the buggy, and resumed holding the reins as the horse slowly plodded forward. She knew the way home after going to town for over five years now. The road dipped and then snaked in and around the grain elevators, five huge monsters lined up in a row like military sentinels. The road took a right turn up ahead before it straightened out once again heading north.

Noah produced two of the apples and handed them back to the girls. He took the third one out and after rubbing it on his vest, took a deep bite.

CHAPTER 8

Faith

Back home, Faith was just setting the table for their noon dinner. Before breakfast, she had placed a spaghetti squash into the big kettle on the stovetop and covered it with water, stoking up the fire in the woodstove and letting it boil for the next hour. It had been sitting in cold water all morning since then after boiling until Faith drained out the water and scooped the flesh out of the two halves of the thick skin into a large cast-iron skillet she had rubbed with bacon grease.

Without refrigeration, though, you could process practically the whole garden into canning jars and store it all in a cool cellar for the coming winter, you were still restricted to eating what was in season or simply going without. That was the thinking behind the tradition of serving creamed celery at weddings. By then, at the end of the fall harvest when the wedding season began, the only fresh crops left were the rows of kale, Brussel sprouts, celery and broccoli to name a few. Not very festive fare for a wedding dinner. The last of those vegetables were gathered in shortly after the first frosts to ensure they wouldn't be frozen solid shortly after. They joined the rest of the bounty in the cellar: red and white potatoes, giant crocks of sauerkraut, butternut, acorn, spaghetti squash, Hubbard and all varieties of squashes, pumpkins, onions, ropes of garlic, and whatever else could be harvested was harvested. Whatever else, what didn't can well was eaten and fare-welled until the next growing season. It would be the end of salads for sure, fresh corn, radishes, and all the other things you only ate raw. Fresh cucumbers became a thing in memory only, now transformed into quart jars of dill pickles, bread and butter pickles, chow chow, relish and sweet Gherkins.

She poured off any remaining water and patted the stringy mass flat in the skillet, topping it with diced tomatoes and then covering that with a pound of raw bacon strips. There was plenty of cold beet salad left over from the bowl she had made the day before. A bread pudding was baking in the oven next to the skillet, which would top off the meal. Freshly whipped cream was staying cool on the sideboard in the kitchen.

Right on time, baby Patience woke up. Faith changed her diaper and settled into the bent wood hickory rocker in the living room to nurse her. It was such a beautiful day. She had opened the windows on the first floor and enjoyed watching the blue curtains dance with each puff of wind. She mentally noted what might need doing in the next hour. The squash and pudding would both be done around the same time; the fire in the wood box would die down about the same time, too, keeping the food warm until Noah came home. Suddenly Faith found herself nodding off. She carefully stood up, the *bobbel* still attached though her eyes were closed, and carried her off to bed. Both were instantly asleep.

That same Saturday morning found Phoebe helping her *mamm* make up gallon jars of dry cereals to see them through the coming months. They planned to make enough for 'the boys' families and Phoebe's little kitchen, too. Both of her brothers were grown with families of their own now, living on parcels of the same property and farmed with their *dat*. They were still called 'the boys' and probably always would be, being *Mamm's* only two boys. Phoebe completed the family. Their parents had married late and were overjoyed that they even had *bobbeli* at all. Each one was a treasure. Each one a miraculous gift from a generous Father above.

"I got everything we'll need from the co-op last week," *Mamm* reminded Phoebe as she set each scalded jar upside down on the linen towel in the dry sink in the kitchen to cool. Counting them once again, she told Phoebe in what order they would tackle each recipe.

"Dry cereal with rice cereal first, then grape nuts, and then we'll do the granola. I've got a new recipe for granola with olive oil and cardamon. It's out of this world. Millie gave me the recipe. Of course, I'll only use Maudie's recipes from *The Budget* for the other two. They are tried and true. No need to improve on those," she continued, chatting to Phoebe as she assembled the bags and jars and boxes of ingredients along the long trestle table in the kitchen. Her largest bread bowl was ready for the first job to be tackled. The index card with the recipe was clipped into the beak of what was supposed to look like a duck that Abe made out of clothespins in first grade years before.

"Twenty-eight cups rolled oats," *Mamm* read.

"Okay, now two cups of honey," she continued. "It's up in the warming oven over there."

Phoebe was busy measuring out the rice cereal. "It's in there, *Mamm*," she announced. "Eight cups. I'll get the vegetable oil. Two and a half cups?" she asked.

"*Ya*. Two pounds shredded sweetened coconut," *Mamm* spoke as she dumped it in.

"Twenty graham crackers," Phoebe counted them.

"But don't crush them, just crumble," *Mamm* ordered.

"I can make this one in my sleep," Phoebe commented. "We've been making this together since I was what, two?"

"*Ya*," *Mamm* chuckled, "and more went in your mouth than in the bowl back then."

"Okay. We only have the sea salt and vanilla extract left. I've got them," *Mamm* said. "Can you get out ten baking sheets? The big ones. And spread it all out in thin layers to bake. We can do three at a time, I figure."

"I've been wondering," *Mamm* began. "What size fruit are those *kinner* now?"

"They are almost grapefruits," Phoebe laughed.

"How can they even tell, all curled up in their feeble position?" she continued.

"Um, *Mamm,* it's called a *fetal* position. FEE'-tal, as in FE-tus," Phoebe explained, trying desperately not to laugh out loud. *Mamm* ignored her, her lips a thin line determined not to reply to such impertinence. *Perhaps I need hearing aids,* Mamm wondered then. *I am thinking I get an awful lot wrong these days....*

With the cereal browning for the next half hour or so in the low oven, or until the coconut turned a golden brown, they began the grape nuts. The first steps made up the thick buttermilk and graham flour mixture that would bake in several loaf pans. Then it would be cut into slabs and dried out in the oven overnight. The next day the slabs were grated and then the 'nuts' or grated bits were toasted again in a low oven till they are brown, dried and crunchy.

CHAPTER 9
Faith

As the horse turned the corner around the last of the three-story high silos at the grain elevator, her right ear twitched. Something was up. She couldn't see it with the square leather blinders cutting off her peripheral vision, so she swung her chest and shoulders enough to be able to look straight at the train bearing down on her, only yards away. She had already stepped onto the tracks with her front hoofs. She reared, emitting an eerie scream, unable to back up with the buggy hardware solidly encasing her torso. The train threw her forward and to the right, flipping the buggy at the same time, which landed squarely upside down on the tracks, another few yards ahead. The train's full impact hit it next, reducing the buggy to millions of shards of wood splinters. The only other sound was a V of geese overhead honking their way north and the shrill screech of the brakes as the engineer gave them as much pull as he dared without derailing the whole train.

It was over in seconds. The train engineer sat there, frozen, his mouth open, his eyes wide. Slowly he disembarked from the cab and stood on the side of the engine, surveying the carnage. "No, oh, no. Dear God, No! Please..." He sat down then on the oily rocks on the side of the tracks and wept into his hands, great sobs of horror and shame. They should have put a railroad sign up long ago. This wasn't the first accident on this corner, though he could already tell it was by far the very worst. Gingerly, partially lifting his hands from his eyes, he peeked out, hoping that what his brain had told him wasn't exactly true. That somehow it was a bad dream. A nightmare. But it was. True. One he had dreaded for years.

The first vehicle to appear on the scene was a pickup truck driven by a local off-duty sheriff. He immediately turned off the ignition and, grabbing his cell phone out of his shirt pocket, dialed 911 as he jumped out of the truck. As he ran to the tracks, he shouted into the phone, "Code red, 10-39, 10-33 repeat, 10-39, 10-33 multiple fatalities, train accident..." and gave the coordinates. He surveyed the wreckage, and his breath caught as he realized he was looking at a child. *No one could have survived this*, he thought to himself. *Didn't the horn on the train go off? That is a blind corner as it is,* he told himself as he continued to grapple with the facts. Nothing moved. He climbed over the debris toward the child. He didn't have to feel for a pulse. It was obvious. He continued to wander around the scene in slow motion and found the father. Also dead. The horse didn't make it either.

Soon the streets on both sides of the tracks were filled with emergency vehicles, ambulances, police cars, sheriffs' cruisers, fire engines and EMTs. The wreckage soon resembled an anthill, with the first responders deftly picking through what was left of the buggy and the family, each doing the job they were trained for while hoping they would never have to use that knowledge, but here they were. Police photographers were taking multiple pictures of each stage of the recovery, while sorting of the refuse was continued late into the night.

The emergency services were reconvened at the local hospital within hours. It was paramount that the family be identified and next of kin be notified as quickly as possible. A wallet with ID had not been found. The father had been foremost in the front of the buggy and suffered fatal, mutilating injuries. A second child had been found as they removed slats of wood and debris that was piled up along the train tracks.

Faith awoke and looked at the clock by her bed. Three o'clock. Where were they? They should have been home hours ago. Had she and Patience been asleep for over two hours at least? She piled pillows on both sides of the sleeping baby on the bed to prevent her from rolling off and stepped into the kitchen. Taking the squash and the bread pudding out of the oven, she threw two hot pads onto the sideboard and let the casserole pan and the iron skillet cool there.

Where are they? she wondered. Maybe they met friends in town and stopped to visit. Ya never know, she concluded. This is a gut time for a cell phone, she reasoned, but told herself she could probably get to heaven without one. Going back into the bedroom, she sat on the bed and folded the mountain of clean diapers in the basket on the floor. Surely, they'd be home soon. At four o'clock, Patience woke up ready to eat again. Faith wrapped her in a light blanket and went out to one of the rockers on the porch that faced the county road. She nursed the happy baby, waiting patiently for the rest of her family to return. Half of life was waiting. 'Life in the slow lane' is what some of the *Amische* youth called it. You get used to it. It did make for a peaceful life. No need to rush. There was always tomorrow and plenty of hands to help if you needed them.

The hospital was a flurry of activity by now. The sheriff was appointed the job of tracking down the Amish and asking how to enlist one of their bishops to help the community with this tragedy.

He drove his cruiser toward Miller's Mercantile. That would be a central place and they had a phone, though he doubted the bishop's home would.

Stepping into the store, he walked up to the counter and found Millie. Millie Miller was a pillar of the community. Close to eighty, she would know everyone and everything happening in the Amish world around them.

"Millie," he began. "There's been a horrible accident. I need your assistance to get a couple of your ministers to help us sort this all out. Can you help us?"

Millie was at once taken aback by this news.

"It's bad then?" she tentatively ventured. He nodded. "How bad?" she asked.

"A buggy was hit by a train this morning over by the feed mill going out of town," he replied.

"Oh, *Gott, no,*" she answered, putting both hands over her mouth. She thought for a moment. "There's a phone shanty over by Bishop Lehman's. We'll try there first. Hope someone hears it though," she said as she dialed the number listed on the yellowed paper taped by the phone next to the cash register on the counter.

"*Ya,*" she shouted into the phone too loudly. "The sheriff here wants to talk to *ya,*" she yelled, handing him the phone.

Within minutes, two buggies rolled up to the store. The sheriff explained the situation to the bishop and his son as they got into the patrol car. The whole scenario was explained to them on the way to the hospital. They were stunned by the story. Surely, they would know whose buggy it was. Too scared to even ask, they didn't raise the question in the car: had anyone died?

At the hospital, they were ushered into a conference room where a team of medical personnel had been assembled. Again, they were told all of the details of the accident that they'd learned so far. Three bodies were in the hospital morgue and in order for them to notify the next of kin, they needed to be identified. Would the bishop be willing to do that?

Of course, he agreed, but dreaded what was being asked of him. He prayed as he followed the doctor down the stairs to the hospital basement. He begged his God to help him be strong. His prayer became more desperate as they neared the place he'd find his own sheep laid out, already having left this earth, their families not even aware yet that they'd fallen asleep in the Lord. This was probably the hardest thing Jesus had ever asked him to do. He begged and pleaded for strength as he entered the cool, sterile room.

Faith was still sitting with Patience on her lap on the porch when the police cars arrived. She could not imagine what they could want. She saw them first out on the road, expecting them to pass by her driveway, but then they turned in and drove up to the house. Then she knew.

She knew this wasn't good news, but she hoped it wasn't any semblance of her worst fear, every Amish person's worst fear: a buggy accident.

But it was. Sitting in the living room with the police and the bishop on the sofa by her side, she heard it all. It couldn't be any worse. Time stopped. Her mind switched to moving in slow motion. She simply couldn't take it all in. Not yet. Perhaps never.

"What do we do now?" was the next thought she was able to form into words while still holding Patience close.

"We'll leave our police liaison here with you. She'll drive you wherever you need to go, to stay with your folks, keep tabs on any developments and keep you updated. Again, we can't tell you how sorry we all are for your loss..." the policeman said, though none of it registered in Faith's mind, refusing to accept any of it just yet. Why? Now? Her whole future ahead of her. Her children's lives, decades certainly, to grow up, marry, have their *kinner.* Take over the farm, care for their parents in their old age. Really? Perhaps she was sleeping, and it was all a terrible nightmare. Was it really their time? Ordained by *Gott?* Was this any of His doing? He is a merciful and kind *Gott.* How could He decide? Why? Why them? She had visions then of wakes she had attended. There were always the elderly who had died peacefully at home, laying so placid in their handmade pine coffins, hands crossed, dressed in white, their sparse hairs combed into place. There was the little boy who had never left his bed, never spoke, who was so very lovingly cared for at home until it was his time, just before his tenth birthday. And then there was the *bruder*, only a teen, who drank too much beer one night during his *rumschpringe* and climbed the grain lag on a dare one windy, wintery night and

52

slipped on the top of the icy ladder falling to his death two-hundred seventy-five feet below.

Her body was shaking now. Someone brought her a cup of tea, which she gratefully sipped after Bishop Lehman took the baby from her and gently bounced the *bobbel* on his knee. Then he offered to bring her parents to the farm to be with her here. Faith could only nod. She'd already surrendered her mind and body to others who seemed to know what to do now. That trust had been instilled since she was born; that belonging to a church *leut,* an *Amische* community, the wider family would take care of its own no matter what. She slowly began the mantra then that would fill her mind in the coming days, though it couldn't really block out the absolute horror of what happened, and it brought little peace and fewer answers just now. *Jesus, son of* Gott, *have mercy on me a sinner....* Yes, she could cling to Him and He would show her the way, though only He knew how it would all get sorted out.

CHAPTER 10
Phoebe

A be showed up unexpectedly at his *Mamm's* door. Phoebe opened the door and announced to *Mamm, "die boova sinn do."* Isaac had gone to get *Dat* from the barn. Phoebe cleared a place at the table among the cereal ingredients they had amassed, brought out a platter of date bars from the pantry and put the coffee on the stove. She still had no idea why they'd suddenly shown up, assuming it was just a good time for a coffee break, and wanted to surprise their parents. When they were all together in the kitchen, Abe began.

"We just heard Noah Stoll was killed this morning with his two older *meedel*. A train hit them at that intersection going north —the one without any signs or bells or a gate—in town. They died instantly."

"Oh, no!" *Mamm* gasped, her eyes suddenly huge.

"How did you find out?" *Dat* whispered.

Isaac answered. "We heard the sirens and seen all the emergency vehicles on the road when we went to check it out."

Then Abe spoke. "I still can't believe it..."

"Oh, poor Faith. I can't imagine, *Mamm,*" Phoebe said as she broke into tears, lifting up the hem of her black apron and sobbing into it.

"Why don't you boys and I take the buggy over to their farm and see if we can help out? We can do the evening milking at least

54

and see how they're fixed over there. I don't want to overwhelm her, but we need to organize this a bit," *Dat* suggested. He drained the last of his coffee and got up, grabbing his straw hat from the peg by the door as he left, the boys following him.

"Oh, *Mamm*. Why?" Phoebe moaned.

"We don't know why these things happen. We must accept it and trust the *gut* Lord. It's hard to bear, though," *Mamm* trailed off into her own thoughts.

"I feel so helpless, *Mamm*. What can we do?" Phoebe asked, wiping her eyes, attempting to gulp down her sobs.

They both sat there then, staring into their coffees, their minds reeling with the news.

"There'll be a funeral tomorrow or the next day. There'll be a meal too. We could start baking, I suppose. Every other *frau* in the district will be doing the same thing, I'm afraid. They lost both girls? Is that right?" *Mamm* questioned Phoebe who could only nod sadly before bursting into tears once more.

"So Faith wasn't with them, or the new *bobbel* I take it," Phoebe puzzled. "How do you even live with something like that?"

The news travelled fast. Dozens of buggies rode to the Stoll farm throughout the late afternoon and into the evening. Faith's parents had been brought to the house and cared for their daughter and her baby. They lit the lamps and pulled chairs into the living room. They sat her down in the kitchen and made her eat what she could of the leftover dinner, followed by sweet tea. Her mother straightened the house and tended to the baby while Faith napped, grateful to fall into the oblivion of sleep where she fleetingly wished she could remain forever after now. Her mind told her she would be cared for, that she didn't have to worry about anything, but at the moment nothing seemed to sink in, much less stick or make sense. She abandoned her body to a deep sleep then, pushing away all the questions and doubts, and the niggling little demons of anger that threatened to push her into what she could only guess would be a dark hole of eternal, raging insanity. *Lord Jesus Christ, have mercy on me,* she begged.

By the next morning, Faith had woken, nursed her baby and let her mother guide her to the kitchen table where she slowly chewed whatever was placed before her without tasting it and drank the sweet coffee they urged on her. The buzz of people talking in low voices all around the house remained unintelligible to Faith's ears. She walked to the outhouse, still in her long nightgown, with her mother who stood at the door and guided her back to the house afterwards. She rocked her hickory rocker in the living room, cradling her sleeping baby, her only connection left to her of her husband. She squashed all questions as they threatened to rear their evil heads in her numb brain and heart: *WHY? Why them? Why now? Couldn't You have prevented it? You can do anything, can't you? But why?... Lord have mercy on me....*

It was safer not to think, not to blaspheme the Lord who in His Eternal Infinite Wisdom ordained all. Who were we to question?

Well-meaning relatives sat by Faith in the living room, offering empty platitudes. How could she believe any of it? It was His Will? They are in a better place? Really? They didn't suffer? She gave Patience to her mother and slowly shuffled back to the bedroom. Too much talking. She wasn't ready. Sleep was the only escape. Blissful rest. *What was that hymn? Leaning, leaning, leaning on the everlasting Arms, leaning, leaning... Oh what joy divine, oh what... a fellowship... Lord have mercy on me...*

CHAPTER 11

Faith

The funeral. Surreal. How could she be sure her family was even in those coffins? She sat where they'd parked her as more and more vans and buggies from far and wide deposited *Amische* at the Plain cemetery.

They'd advised against Faith viewing the bodies. Her *kinner* and *der mann* weren't there. Their bodies had been practically destroyed by the crash. "They are in *Gott's* heaven where we will all see them again one day," she had been assured repeatedly. She couldn't protest. How could she rail against a *Gott* so powerful, so wise while she was only a mere *frau?*

She clasped little Patience tighter against her chest. Blessed consolation. She still had Patience, though this *Gott* apparently had every right to take her too, should He choose to. *For shame! Quiet!* she silently admonished her thoughts. Better not to have any than sin against the Lord. More platitudes. The sermons were full of them. "Our way... accept what He deems we are able to carry... never sends us more than we can bear... His Ways are not our ways...."

Faith wished she were home already, napping, the only relief she'd found so far. *Does time really heal? I don't believe it,* she bitterly questioned and then answered herself. *No, I will be like this forever. There's no escape. How do you ever forgive* Gott? *I will be damned. I won't see them in heaven after all. It would have been better if I had been in that buggy, too. At least I wouldn't be here blaspheming* Gott. *Oh, Lord Jesus, have mercy.... Even my name is a bad joke—Faith.*

The final hymn sung in the living room before the last visitors left that first evening could not have been more appropriate. Its author, Horatio Spafford, lost four young daughters when the ship *Ville du Havre* sank in the Atlantic on its way to France in November 1873. Faith would not have realized it that day, but one day it would bring her some semblance of courage. Her faith would also return, but not yet. She would wander through this dark valley of death for more days to come.

> When peace like a river, attendeth my way,
> When sorrows like sea billows roll;
> Whatever my lot, Thou hast taught me to know
> It is well, it is well, with my soul.

> *Refrain*
> It is well, (it is well),
> With my soul, (with my soul)
> It is well, it is well, with my soul.

> Though Satan should buffet, though trials should come,
> Let this blest assurance control,
> That Christ has regarded my helpless estate,
> And hath shed His own blood for my soul.

> My sin, oh, the bliss of this glorious thought!
> My sin, not in part but the whole,
> Is nailed to the cross, and I bear it no more,
> Praise the Lord, praise the Lord, O my soul!

> For me, be it Christ, be it Christ hence to live:
> If Jordan above me shall roll,
> No pang shall be mine, for in death as in life,
> Thou wilt whisper Thy peace to my soul.

> But Lord, 'tis for Thee, for Thy coming we wait,

The sky, not the grave, is our goal;
Oh, trump of the angel! Oh, voice of the Lord!
Blessed hope, blessed rest of my soul.

And Lord, haste the day when faith shall be sight,
The clouds be rolled back as a scroll;
The trump' shall resound, and the Lord shall descend,
A song in the night, oh my soul!

CHAPTER 12

Ezra & Edith

Another *Samschdaag.* Edith and Ezra were tidying the house as they expected Ruth and her family to come for Hannah Rose any time now. Edith found herself crying while she changed the baby's diapers.

"What am I going to do without you?" she asked the chubby little girl as the tears landed on her pudgy legs. "Maybe they'll let me keep you. Maybe just for a bit longer?" The baby kicked and wiggled, laughing as Edith wrestled her into the diaper.

She hefted Hannah Rose off the bed and set her on the floor, picking Howard up next to change his diaper, too.

"What are we going to do without her, Howard?" Edith continued, tears continuing to fall on him now. "I know, you'll miss her too, won't you?"

Ezra walked into the bedroom then. "They'll be here soon, honey. Now try to act happy, please? We've done a *gut* thing helping them out this way. We should be glad her *mamm* is better now, eh?"

"You're right. I will miss her something terrible, though," she said as the tears she had just managed to contain threatened to return. She set Howard down on the floor where he stood, wobbling, holding onto the corner of the bed and quickly, though haltingly, followed Hannah Rose where she also stood and then took off around the bed.

"Look at that!" Ezra marveled, chuckling. "Their first steps."

They each grabbed a *bobbeli* and headed out to the yard. The family sat under the big oak tree, waiting for the old rickety station wagon to appear and groan its way up the driveway.

Soon they saw the old car wheezing its way up the gravel drive. The four children were the first to burst out of it and run to their little sister who didn't register at all at first who all these wild *kinner* were. Edith looked up to see Ruth looking quite pale as she asked if she could lie down in the house for a bit. The surgery had only been three weeks earlier and that long car ride had not been very kind on her stomach. Edith jumped up and led Ruth to the bedroom, bringing her a glass of water.

"Thank you so much. I'll be okay in a bit," she mumbled, her eyes closed as Edith sat down on the bed next to her.

"We could keep her a bit longer if you like," Edith offered. "Till you're stronger, maybe?" she asked hopefully.

"I should be okay. David will be home for a few more days and some friends will chip in, too. I can't thank you enough, though. I didn't have to worry about her. The others seemed to have weathered it okay too," Ruth added before taking another sip. "I'm just glad the surgery is over and I won't have to worry about passing out and hemorrhaging again. I'm sad that's the end of having babies, but I have to be able to raise the ones I've got now, you know," she reasoned, still trying to convince herself she had no other choice.

"Can't I keep her?" Edith suddenly blurted out, the tears reappearing in full force.

"What?" Ruth said as she struggled to sit up.

"You have all the others. We love her so much. Can I keep her?" Edith begged.

"Oh, Edith. I am so sorry. I didn't realize. I'm sorry," Ruth said as she held Edith's hand. "I'm so sorry. I can't," was all Ruth could say then.

"I know," Edith said, surrendering to her grief. She sobbed into her handkerchief then as Ruth reached out and hugged her, her own tears mingling with Hannah Rose's other *mamm's*.

When they had both recovered somewhat, they walked out to

the yard with the Tupperware box of cookies Edith had made the day before. When all the children were quietly devouring the soft Whoopie Pies, David handed Ezra an envelope. Apologetically, he said, "It isn't very much. I wish we had more, but we wanted to thank you. You have no idea what a help this was. Thank you two so much," he said. "You three, actually," he added and looked at Howard who was oblivious to the fact that they were there to take away his dear little friend as he mushed the soft cookie into his mouth.

Ezra nodded, embarrassed by the gift, the fact being that he'd never expected to be paid. As David buckled all the children into the car, the little family stood by the tree, waving goodbye. Ezra was holding Howard who began to wail as his little friend disappeared into the back seat. Edith's tears also began rushing down her cheeks once again. As the car disappeared down the road, the little family returned to the farmhouse to try to rebuild their lives to what it had been before Hannah Rose came to them, if that were even possible. But the Lord had seen their anguish and their tears. In only another week, they would guess correctly that they had another *bobbel* on the way, a little girl they would name Hannah Rose.

CHAPTER 13

Faith

I n the following days, Faith was surrounded by others who did understand her loss. Story after story was told at that long kitchen table of children lost, of husbands taken too early. Faith listened, barely grasping each tale, but slowly she could hear them and began to absorb the fact that she wasn't alone, that they did indeed understand, that she didn't have to instantly forgive and forget. That was *not* being asked of her. That if the community surrounding her could give her time and space to heal—all the time she needed—then so would *Gott*.

Her *Grossmammi* sat with her in the kitchen rocking Patience while Faith ate the warm oatmeal her *Mammi* had fixed for her. Her mother was puttering around the house while she knew her *dat* and other men and boys were seeing to the chores in the barn. She didn't even have to know who was out there. She was just reassured that they were there and had come every day, twice a day faithfully to see to things since the beginning.

The beginning. The first day of the rest of her life, and the last day of What Had Been, the time before. That old life that was gone now. The months carrying each of those *bobbeli* inside of her... Their births, hard but again assured they would be safely delivered. Then nursing each one past their first and then second birthdays. The years before that, getting to know Noah, his family, his *mamm* and *dat*. Then starting the farm. The

63

struggle to pay off the loans, the frugal years putting aside every penny to make it work, simplifying their meals even further if that were at all possible, most suppers back then consisting of canned tomato soup and soggy Ritz crackers. Then the blessings of new calves, broody chickens raising dozens of chicks, finally making their own butter and cheese. Their first colt born on the farm. The acres of alfalfa being added each year. Sleeping next to your love each night, completely worn out but happy. Fulfilled. Faith could not imagine ever having such feelings again. She felt cold. Dead. Numb. Unfeeling.

"You don't have to forget," *Mammi* said and then waited, letting that sink in.

Faith looked up at her, puzzled. *I don't just forgive and forget?* she questioned herself.

Mammi repeated it. "You don't have to forget. You never will. You just bring them along with you now. They are still with you, Faith. They will always be a part of you."

Faith slowly sucked the oatmeal off the spoon, trying to understand what this meant. No one had proposed this one yet. It was staggering. A new thought. She had been begging *Gott* every minute of every day and every night to have mercy on her and give her that elusive grace: forgiveness. She believed she had been fighting against forgiveness ever since she'd learned of the accident and that the reason she wasn't finding any peace was because she was somehow refusing to forgive *Gott*. How could He? How could He do this to one of His own? He wasn't even giving her the wherewithal that was promised to bear all things. It wasn't being given to *her*, at least. She would spend eternity in Hell for her sin, she had convinced herself. This wasn't life now. It was her punishment, perhaps her Purgatory. No, she told herself, this was actually already Hell. *Gott* had forsaken her.

Looking at *Mammi* again, her mind swam in circles. Nothing made sense. It was better not to think. All hope was gone. It couldn't possibly return again. Along with her precious Hope and Charity. Gone. Noah gone too. Everything she'd ever held dear. Is that why they'd been taken? That she hadn't appreciated them enough, taken it all for granted? Divine retribution on some cosmic scale?

The days dragged on. Cakes, pies, casseroles, jars of canned goods, baskets of fruit, and loaves of bread appeared on the kitchen table at all hours of the day and into the evenings. Faith had not been forgotten. No one challenged her choice to cease all conversation. When asked how she was doing, all she could do was shrug her shoulders and look away. She didn't even know how she was doing. She wished she wasn't 'doing' at all. The thought of running away in the middle of the night and throwing herself on those same train tracks had entered her mind more than once, though she quickly turned to prayer, falling on her knees by her bed onto the cold floor in those fleeting moments and begging *Gott* for mercy.

While wandering aimlessly through the house the next day, she ventured into the *dawdi haus* next to the kitchen where her husband's father had lived, until he passed away two years earlier. Looking into the bathroom cupboard, she realized they hadn't cleaned it out, and it was still full of all his medications from that time.

She picked up the little wicker trash basket from below the sink and began filling it with the half-empty bottles. Then it occurred to her. A sedative would be nice. Surely no one would begrudge her that.

She quickly rummaged back through the bottles and found what she was looking for. She could take just enough to dull the pain, but not enough to hurt herself. Just a few so she could sleep and forget, just for a while. That wouldn't be a sin, would it?

She scanned the rest of the bottles, separating out the ones she thought might help and carried those to her bedroom, carefully lining them up under the 'unmentionables' in her top drawer —her mother's name for her underthings. Maybe she would find some escape from the constant doubts and fears. How could her own mind be her worst enemy at this point? Feeling nothing, being numb was better than this roller coaster ride. *Lord have mercy*...she prayed. Had He forsaken her? Why had she not been given the grace to come through her grief? It was all so unfair.

She couldn't even cry anymore. Time to take something, anything and curl up under the covers once again. Patience would be fine for a few more hours with her *Grossmammi* watching her in the other room...*have mercy on me a miserable sinner.* And then...blessed sleep.

Mammi brought the *bobbel* into Faith's room and laid her next to Faith on the bed. She called, gently shook her shoulder, and wiped back the hairs falling over her face while calling her name again. Faith didn't even grunt in return. Then she saw it. The medicine bottle on the nightstand. Picking it up, she read the label. *Morphine extended-release capsules. No doctor has given this to her,* she told herself. *Ach Faith, what are you doing, honey pie?*

Mammi shook her harder this time and helped arrange Patience next to her *mamm,* so she could nurse. Faith briefly opened one eye and wrapped a protective arm around the baby, pulling her close.

Mammi ran out into the living room where Faith's sister Gracie was reading *The Budget.*

Mammi ordered her, "Quick. Go get that nurse, the Schwartz girl. We need her. Take the buggy and hurry! Now!"

Mammi returned to the bedroom and pulled a chair up to the bed. She wasn't going to leave Faith alone, not now. Not for a second. Picking up the bottle, she realized they had been prescribed to Noah's father who lived with them before he died peacefully in his sleep. Then *Mammi* jumped up and went to the dresser, opened the drawers and rifled around until she found the rest of the bottles. *How long have you been doing this, Faithie?*

Returning to her post, *Mammi* picked up the baby and hoisted her up on her shoulder. She was instantly rewarded with a burp. She changed the *bobbel's* diaper and sat back in the chair, whispering little kisses into the baby's ear. Patience waved her arms and cooed back. *Grossmammi* felt Faith's neck for a pulse and noted the pink cheeks and the steady rise and fall of her chest. She was sure she was breathing, but what would she do if that stopped? *Mammi* prayed that wouldn't happen until help came. *Lord have mercy,* she begged. *Help us here, please, sweet Jesus...*

Within an hour, *Mammi* heard the buggy's metal-rimmed wheels screeching and crunching on the gravel in the driveway. Still holding the baby, she went into the kitchen as Phoebe walked in, removing her shoes on the mat by the door. *Mammi* sat down, and Phoebe followed. Gracie just behind her stood against the stove.

"How can I help? Is the *bobbel* sick? Is Faith okay?" she began. Luckily, it was a no-church Sunday, and she wasn't away at school today either. Both would have made it very hard to find her.

Reaching across the table, *Mammi* took the morphine bottle and placed it in front of Phoebe.

"There's more. She had a bunch in a drawer. I'm afraid she's taken some. I couldn't wake her up before. She's still sleeping now. Why would anyone do such a thing? Do you think she was trying to kill herself?" *Mammi's* eyes filled with tears that fell onto the baby's downy head and then her hands as she was nervously twisting the hem of the baby blanket.

Phoebe jumped up and ran into the bedroom. Observing Faith's regular breathing and then taking her pulse told her she wasn't in any imminent danger. Returning to the kitchen she picked up and opened the bottle. There were at least a dozen pills still in there.

"I don't think so," Phoebe began, answering *Mammi's* last question. "She didn't take all of it, so we're lucky there. My guess is that she was self-medicating to dull the pain of this last week, maybe longer. It isn't uncommon, but she needs help. I think I can get the doctor to make a house call and we can figure this one out. Don't leave the baby with her, though. If she is drugged up, she could roll on her without knowing it. I'm going to go out to the phone shanty by the barn and make a few calls. We'll figure this out. I promise."

Phoebe stopped then and turned back to *Mammi*. "We'll watch the baby, too. I'm not sure how safe it is to breastfeed with this stuff on board. We'll sort it out, either way," she said as she went out, but not before noting that the baby was wide awake and happily cooing, deep in conversation with the lamp that was hanging above her in the kitchen.

The phone operator agreed to stay on the line to assist Phoebe with as many calls as she needed to make after she had explained the emergency. The doctor was home and more than willing to come out. He would be there as soon as he could. Phoebe gave him the address and the street coordinates before thanking him for helping them.

Back in the house, *Mammi* gave Patience to Phoebe to hold while she fixed the evening meal. When Gracie had suddenly turned up at Phoebe's house, saying they needed her but that she had no idea why *Mammi* had sent for her, Phoebe told her *Mamm* not to hold supper for her and let Stephen know, too. She would stay as long as they needed her, even overnight if warranted.

Returning to the bedroom, Phoebe peeked in to see Faith still sleeping and breathing evenly. She wondered if she was overstepping her protocols by not calling for an ambulance. She had made an executive decision not to, given the circumstances she found herself in, but now began to doubt if it was the right one. If Faith became suddenly worse, or the *bobbel* stopping breathing, she'd be held responsible. For the next hour she paced the kitchen floor, bouncing the happy baby on her hip while plumbing her brain to recall any guidelines that she'd learned at nursing school that could or should be applied in this situation. Continuing to come up short in that department, she checked on Faith periodically, returning to the kitchen to reassure *Mammi* that the doctor would be able to help as soon as he arrived.

Giving the baby back to *Mammi*, Phoebe looked at the wall clock in the kitchen and calculated how long ago Faith could have taken the dose that she did. It was three o'clock when Gracie got to the farm. That would have taken her less than half an hour to get there. More like twenty minutes. Driving back to the farm would be the same. One hour tops. Phone shanty, another half an hour out and back combined at the most. Walking the baby, now it was almost five o'clock. And she had been already asleep when *Mammi* found the pills. She plunked the happy baby in the cradle in the kitchen where she could watch her *mammi*. Finding a clean dish rag in a cupboard above the kitchen sink, Phoebe soaked it in water and wrung it out. Walking back into the bedroom, she gently rocked Faith's shoulder until she roused her. She quickly sat Faith up and wiped her face and neck with the cold rag while talking to her. "Let's get you up and to the loo," she quietly insisted. Faith obediently stood and let Phoebe take her hand and lead her out the house's back door and the few feet to the outhouse. Returning to the kitchen, Phoebe sat Faith down as *Mammi* pushed a mug of sweet, creamy coffee in front of her. Faith's eyes were still closed as Phoebe helped her hold the mug in both hands and brought it up to her lips where she began sipping it.

Mammi checked on Patience in the cradle in the corner of the kitchen and returned to the stove to slowly stir the soup. A bowl of crackers were soaking in milk on the table along with the soup bowls and spoons. A Shoo-fly pie brought only that morning by one of their faithful neighbors who delivered food to the house every day—rain or shine—was sitting on the table along with a small bowl of whipped cream.

Mammi served the thick tomato soup and sat down next to Faith. She plopped a large spoonful of the soggy crackers into the bowl of soup, stirring it. Faith opened her eyes halfway as she caught a whiff of the food before her. Lifting the spoon by her bowl, she began eating, oblivious to her surroundings and the addition of Phoebe to the house. So many people had been coming and going these last few days that it didn't really matter anymore who or how many had taken over her life as she had known it before... before the.... Faith was suddenly reminded of the stark facts once again. Placing both hands squarely on the edge of the table, she attempted to get up, hoping to find her way back to the soft cocoon where she could forget it all.

Phoebe helped her sit back down, gently talking to her, suggesting she finish the soup first, feed the baby again and maybe take a bath, too. *Mammi* had already noted Faith's unwashed odor earlier in the day and had the large canning kettle boiling on the back of the stove for a bath. They finished their supper, plying Faith with a slice of pie smothered in cream, which she didn't object to. The fact was that she didn't have any fight left in her. None at all. Her only wish was to fade into oblivion, forgetting everything. Sleep forever. Blessed sleep.

The bath was soothing, too. *Mammi* washed Faith's hairs, combing out the snags with Tea Tree Conditioner and scrubbed her back with the large loofah sponge. Phoebe found a clean flannel nightgown in the bedroom and helped Faith into it. They led her to the rocker in the living room where they plopped Patience into her lap, essentially making her a prisoner, just as they heard a car door close.

Phoebe ran out to talk with the doctor as *Mammi* sat down on the sofa next to Faith's chair.

The doctor followed Phoebe into the kitchen where she silently pointed to the pill bottles on the sideboard as they walked through to the living room. He stopped to read the labels, nodding to himself as he calculated how many pills were probably still in each bottle and how much would push someone over the edge, compromising their breathing or heart function.

Coming into the living room, he sat down next to *Mammi*.

"Hi, Faith. Can you see me? Open your eyes," he ordered, though gently, quietly. She did, her eyes scanning the room for this unfamiliar voice.

"Hi. I'm here by your grandmother. I'm a doctor. How are you doing? Phoebe asked me to come by and check on you," he said.

"Uh huh," was her bland answer as she closed her eyes once again.

"How are you?" he insisted.

Faith shut her lips tight, deciding it wasn't up to this stranger to know how she was. *She* didn't even know how she was. It was just too painful. She didn't want to have to think and put her feelings into any perspective. Maybe she could just crawl back to bed and be done with this interview.

"Faith, it looks like you aren't managing very well, and we all want to help you. Everyone is concerned about you, and I think we can support you here a little better. Is that okay?" he asked.

"You don't know," was her curt answer, eyes still shut.

"No, I don't. I can only imagine. But there are some ways to help you get through this."

"Time will heal this...they are in a better place...you can have more babies...I've heard it all. They don't have a clue. *You* don't have a clue. Nothing can fix this." Faith's voice and bitter words trailed off. She shut her eyes once again, hoping to shut out the whole waking world.

"No, those things people say don't help, do they? But it sounds like you are depressed, maybe seriously depressed and I want to suggest a few things here that we can start and see if we can get you in a better place. Will you be willing to try to work with us?" he asked.

Faith looked at him then. Really looked at him, glowering. Then *Mammi* spoke, "Faith, Patience needs you. We all need you. Please just listen. Just try, darling, okay?"

"I dunno," she replied, closing her eyes once again and gripping the arms of the rocker till her knuckles turned white.

Phoebe spoke next. "We're thinking we should put together a plan here to help you feel better. You can't take your *doddy's* pills any more, Faith. They could hurt you and Patience, too. It's understandable that you are depressed. No one should have to go through what you've been through. We're going to support you better here. Some appropriate meds will help. So will eating better and sleeping more regularly. We'll make sure someone is here with you, too, like they've been. You can get through this, but you'll need help for a while. How does that sound?"

"Mmm," was Faith's noncommittal reply.

Then *Mammi* spoke. "I think this sounds *gut*. Please just try it?"

Still quite sleepy, Faith managed the slightest nod in agreement.

The doctor got up and brought a cup of water back from the kitchen and offered it with the first of the pills he prescribed. "This will definitely help," he assured her. "Your family will make sure you take these at the proper times. I promise you will start to feel a whole lot better soon."

"Uh huh," Faith managed sleepily, still unconvinced that anything could help, much less a tiny happy pill or two.

Phoebe met him in the kitchen before he left. She handed him the wicker basket with all the pills she had managed to find.

"Can you get rid of these?" she asked him.

He nodded. "Please call me any time if you have questions. Any time at all. Let's see how this goes, okay?"

Phoebe nodded, taking the new pill bottle from him.

"I'm so glad you were here," he added, turning back from the kitchen door. "This helps me tremendously. You have no idea. Really." Phoebe said a silent prayer then thanking *Gott* for this good doctor.

Mammi went back to fixing hot cocoa in the kitchen while Phoebe sat with Faith who was nursing Patience again. When Phoebe lifted the baby up, she burped right on cue.

"She is such a sweet baby, Faith. And you are such a *gut mamm*. She's going to need you. You have to get well for her, eh?"

Faith nodded, still unconvinced, feeling only the bitter taste left in her mouth and the bitter pain in her heart.

"Did you know we're expecting?" Phoebe asked.

Faith turned and looked at her and shook her head. "Are you excited?" she asked, her words slurred slightly.

"Very," Phoebe answered. "And we just found out we're having twins. That part is pretty scary. I don't know what that'll be like. Double trouble they say. But it's a secret, okay?"

"Oh, I don't know," Faith pondered that a minute. "I don't want to lose Patience, too," she said then, dissolving into sobs once again.

Phoebe held her in a tight hug. "Shhh...shhh," she whispered. "It's okay. You aren't going to lose her."

Just then, *Mammi* came in with the four mugs on a tray and set it down on the little table in front of the sofa. Taking Patience, she sat down and offered Faith and Gracie each a mug of hot cocoa.

Just then, they heard a buggy coming up to the house. Phoebe ran to the kitchen door and opened it just as her parents came into the room.

"We thought we'd come by and see how you are doing, *Mamm* said, her eyebrows raised as high as they would go while trying to sound cheery, but coming across a bit too animated, obviously not wanting to appear overly concerned, though she was deeply worried. She didn't know exactly why Gracie had whisked Phoebe away earlier in the day, but it didn't bode well, her saying it was an emergency of some kind.

"*Kumm* in," Phoebe invited them, smiling.

"Faith, my *mamm* and *dat* stopped by," Phoebe informed her.

"Oh, look at this baby! How she's grown," *Mamm* gushed, taking the *bobbel* onto her lap.

Then Dat spoke, turning to Faith's grandmother. "We thought I could take you back home and Phoebe's *mamm* could stay the night.

"Oh, that would be gut. *Denke,*" *Mammi* agreed.

"Then *Mamm* and I will stay over. Is that okay, Faith?" Phoebe asked.

"Sure," Faith finally replied blandly. *I don't care. I will never care...* she told herself. *You'll all do whatever you want, anyway. That's what you're doing now. Doping me up with pills, controlling what I think....*

Dat added, "I'll take your *Mammi* and Gracie home tonight and come by again tomorrow."

"Perfect," Phoebe agreed.

"I'll get ready, then," *Mammi* said, getting up.

When they were gone, Phoebe and *Mamm* puttered about the house and then got Faith into bed. The *bobbel* slept in a bassinet next to the big bed.

"I had a thought, Faith. Would it be okay if I slept with you here? The bed is plenty big enough and I can help if Patience wakes up," Phoebe proposed.

"Yes. I'd like that," Faith agreed. Then, allowing her eyes to open just a bit, she offered the smallest hint of a shy smile. *"Denke,"* she whispered.

"I'll get ready then," Phoebe said as she headed toward the

kitchen. She filled *Mamm* in on the plan, pointing out that the only pills in the house were now safely in her own apron pocket.

"Thank you so much for *kumming*. I think things will start looking up now. I sure hope so," Phoebe added.

Mamm made herself comfortable in the adjacent bedroom, lighting the lamp on the dresser and turning back the covers on the double bed there. She slowly walked around the room that the two little girls had shared. Two faceless, though obviously well-love, well-worn dolls sat between the two pillows. Though some families gave their children dolls they'd found at thrift stores, making Amish clothes for them, many preferred the homemade ones, made without faces, only blank muslin under the tiny black bonnets in accordance with the biblical mandate not to make graven images of any kind. That held also for photographs. The dolls were dressed just like their little *mamms* would have been, with long dresses covered with a matching pinafore; four buttons down the back of each dress, a single button securing the pinafore at the top of the back at the neck. One tiny dress and pinafore set was plum-colored and the other a sage green. Both so lovingly made, maybe hand sewn by Faith or her *mamm* or *mammi*. Each a labor of love for a tiny girl that held so very much hope for the future, years ahead of her to grow, outgrow dolls, fall in love and then make dolls for her own little girls.

Mamm's tears fell then as she gazed at the dolls. *Didn't He promise to wipe every tear away? Mamm* asked herself. *Couldn't you start with Faith? Now? Please?*

Mamm continued walking around the bedroom. The pegs along one wall held several small dresses in a rainbow of colors: pink, lavender, dark blue, teal, purple, and light blue, a sweater for each, little starched black church *kapps,* and two miniature wool shawls. Two little handmade nightgowns were folded and sat on a chair in the corner of the room now bathed in shadows. A wicker basket below the pegs held carefully rolled pairs of socks along with a little covered wagon that had obviously lost its team somewhere along the way.

On top of the short dresser by the door, a small herd of plastic horses assembled, a few cows thrown in for good measure, the leaded glass mirror behind multiplying their numbers. Two birthday cards were taped to the mirror, more horses galloping through fields of hay pictured there on each card.

By each side of the bed, a small round crocheted rug sat. On both rugs a pair of homemade carpet slippers stood, patiently waiting for little feet to return to them, which never would now.

Taking a deep breath as she walked back to the master bedroom, *Mamm* found Phoebe ready for bed, too.

"We'll have our prayers here then," *Mamm* announced.

Faith opened her eyes, unfolded her legs, and got out from under the covers. She knelt with them and, folding her hands, she leaned on the edge of the bed, closed her eyes, bowed her head, and allowed *Mamm*'s and Phoebe's prayers to suffice for her. She couldn't think of what to say after she'd silently exhausted the rote prayers she had learned and said every night of her life thus far but patiently waited on her knees for the others to finish.

Lord have mercy... and Denke, ended her attempt at prayer that night.

Part Two

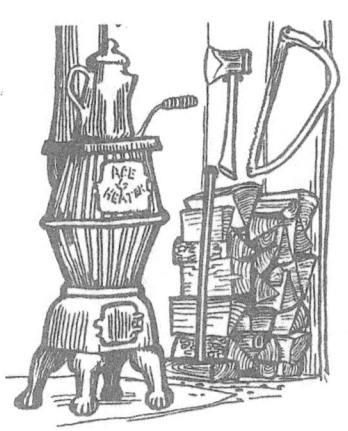

CHAPTER 14

Ben

JESUS IS THE WAY, THE TRUTH, AND THE LIFE... READ
JOHN 14:6.

The sign said it all.

The families who lived in the houses behind these signs mounted on their mailboxes took the Bible seriously, seven days a week, twenty-four hours a day. Of course, they weren't perfect. They were human, but they kept their eyes on the prize and woke up each day with fresh resolve and a prayer on their lips. They strengthened one another and found joy and purpose to forge on.

Ben had been baptized into this flock last Sunday. His heart swelled with peace and freedom. Sure there were rules, both written and unwritten, hundreds of years of translation and interpretation and misinterpretations, but there wasn't the blind, moralistic faith of his birth family, where to doubt was a sin in its own rite.

Where one just accepted all without question because it has always been done that way, and in the end because it was simply 'The Amish Way.' That was how his parents had interpreted the teachings at least, and, as if that weren't hard enough, added a few of their own along the way, instilling a very *un*-forgiving path to follow for their children.

A hard life, almost devoid of all joy, as if enjoying this life and not putting all hope in the next alone was a sin, too, and one Ben no longer felt yoked to. He knew he wasn't learn-ed, and that he didn't possess the intellect of the ministers, but he'd grown to love and trust this new family and didn't feel that what they believed was such a heavy burden to shoulder. It felt more like they carried it together, lightening the load for all.

And he loved Leah, with all his heart. He was sure after his awkward, foolish attempts to court Phoebe that there couldn't possibly be anyone left on earth who might want him. He'd decided back then that it wasn't even the remotest of possibilities. He'd always be a dreamer. A bachelor dreamer, for sure. How could he make anyone happy? He obviously didn't have it in him. No, he would grow old with only the cows for friends, the daily grind his only diversion. Chop wood. Muck out the horse stalls. Cut the hay. Turn the compost. Milk the cows, bring in the hay. Fix fences. Plant the garden and weed it while getting eaten alive by mosquitoes. Shovel the walks. Up at 4:30. To bed with the last rays of the sun. Look after *Mamm* who would only get more ornery as the years went on, dumping more and more of her frustrations on him.

Dat getting older and still just placating her. Was this all there was in this life? He had wondered back then what the purpose of it all was. He was certainly in the doldrums that year. *Dat* had been a big help, encouraging Ben, but he couldn't find him a wife or promise his *mamm* would be kinder. Was this the sum total of his faith? It wasn't the fruits of the Spirit he'd heard about on all those Sundays, stretching back as far as he could remember. When did it all go off track? Was everyone this despondent, but just better at putting on a happy face? Finding a way just to be resigned and not complain? Gosh, but this life wasn't easy, and he didn't see how his prayers were helping either back then.

Leah was helping her *Oma* out of the bath. Her grandmother was almost ninety and recovering at home from surgery for a broken hip. Leah felt honored to be asked to help the sweet old woman. She wrapped a fluffy towel around the skinny shoulders and helped Oma out of the tub, leading her to the office chair they used in leu of a wheelchair. The chair's caster wheels worked perfectly on the linoleum floors that had been laid throughout the house when it was built. She had covered the chair with another towel. When Oma was settled, she took a third towel and started rubbing her hairs dry. She was just finishing up the winter semester at school, looking forward to the final stretch ahead. Then she would be a real nurse.

Her mom was busy in the kitchen, fixing breakfast for the third time that day. The first had been at six a.m. for her husband, and oldest son, who were off to the lumberyard where they worked. The second breakfast was for the three littlest children, Yosef, Yacob, and Simon who had a school bus to catch in less than thirty minutes. They wolfed down the loaded oatmeal and impatiently waited for their mother's obligatory inspection, lining up at the back door. She patted down cowlicks, swiped the corner of her apron across a nose here, a mouth there, and proceeded to button three top buttons that had somehow just found their way to being undone, revealing little chests not even old enough to sprout a single hair, though they secretly harbored that wish.

"Okay, off you go," she finally said, kissing three soft cheeks on their way out, handing each one a tin lunch box. Clearing the table once again, she set it for the third time for *Oma,* Leah and herself. This final setting would be the last for today, at least until supper time when they'd all reconvene. A hasty lunch of sandwiches for Oma and herself would suffice for lunch. Hilda's father would be picking up Leah soon and take the girls to the college.

Leah helped direct the walker to the table and got *Oma* comfortably seated on the office chair once again, that was sporting a feather pillow on the seat. Rolling it up to the table, Leah sat down too.

"This is nice, huh?" she said, pouring cream into her grandmother's coffee. "We're getting our final project papers back today. Wish me luck," she told the others.

"I'm sure you'll get a good grade," her mother said. "That was a huge undertaking. I don't know that I could have managed all that."

"I'm just glad it's done, is all," Leah said after grace.

"Shall we invite Ben to dinner tonight?" her mom asked.

"Yes, please. Would you call over there? Mmm, this is good," she said, changing the subject. "Let me guess, uh, apples, raisins, cinnamon, walnuts, tahini, honey and, um, uh, what is it? Oh, carob chips?" Leah guessed, as she added more cream to her bowl.

"That's right. It'll stick to their ribs till lunch," her mother answered.

"It's very good," *Oma* agreed.

They finished their breakfast just as they heard the car arrive. Kissing her *Oma* and her mother goodbye, Leah flew out the door with her book bag to the waiting car.

"Hiya," Leah said, practically falling into the back seat. "How are you?"

"Good," Hilda answered. "I could have slept longer. Maybe I'm anemic. I'm so tired."

Leah suggested, "You know, some iron and vitamins wouldn't hurt you. My mom insisted and I think it's helping me."

"Okay. I'll get some. How is Ben?" Hilda asked.

"Great. The minister is suggesting the second Sunday of next month for the wedding," she informed Hilda. "I think back to last year when I met him. Can you believe it?"

"Our prayers were answered," Hilda's father replied at that point from the front seat. "We've all been praying for God's will in this from the very beginning."

"Aw, thank you," Leah said, continuing to marvel at the miracle of it all. She, too, had questioned God concerning her future before meeting Ben. What if after college she found that boys were hesitant to date her because they imagined she'd become smarter than they were? Would they feel intimidated by that? Very few Mennonite boys went to college. They were so very skilled in all the trades being passed down from all those generations. Did God want her to serve in the missions, now that she had been gifted with this entire education, all paid for by her church? Would she be expected to somehow give back for all the expense and support? Perhaps being a nurse was a calling in itself, precluding marriage and family? She could certainly fill a lifetime by serving her community. Would God find her a husband, or would another calling become clear? *How does one discern such things?* she asked herself.

They arrived then at the college and sprinted toward the entrance, waving goodbye to Hilda's dad. They had a few minutes to spare, so the two headed to the classroom where they found Phoebe and Susanna.

The first question from everyone was, "how is Faith doing?"

"Better," Phoebe began. "I think we can see light at the end of the tunnel. Last week was pretty scary, but there's been significant improvement, I'd say. Everyone's been so helpful and that doctor is a real gem. I'd say we're lucky it wasn't worse, that we got there in time. Her *mammi* was the one that clicked that something was up."

Just then, the teacher entered the room and class began.

Leah's father picked Ben up from the Brennemans' where he'd been rooming. Ben thought it was just to bring him to supper, but when Dad turned left instead of right, he knew something was up. *Should I ask? Would that be rude? Wonder where we're goin'. Guess I should just trust, huh?* Ben told himself. A short time later, they turned into a driveway. A tiny house with gingerbread trim sat in a little yard surrounded by a white picket fence. Overgrown bushes lined the front of the little house, frozen in time by the hard frost earlier that day. Turning off the van, Leah's dad asked Ben, "Well, what do you think?"

Ben wasn't sure what was 'up' so he just shrugged and was left sitting there with his usual clueless, goofy smile on his face.

"Okay. Just follow me then," Leah's dad said, chuckling.

He pulled a key out of his pocket and unlocked the front door. They both stepped inside.

"I rented it for you and Leah. There's the option to buy, too. It's not far from work or our place, and you can pay us back a little each month," he said as he handed Ben the key.

"I don't know what to say, oh...oh my goodness," Ben stammered.

"It's a good starter home. You two can look around the area and decide on something bigger down the road, but this is a real bargain. Look around. Mom and I really liked it," he explained as Ben walked around the darling little home.

"Does Leah know yet?" Ben asked, returning to the front room.

"No. I thought maybe you'd like to tell her," Dad replied, smiling.

"Oh, wow, sure. I can't wait," Ben answered.

"You can take the car after supper tonight if you want," Dad said. They walked around the house, looking into each room, each closet, and the compact galley kitchen. Leah's mom had already sewed curtains for the windows, each room with a different color scheme. She knew Leah would be busy until she graduated and definitely not have any time to sew curtains for the little cottage. The crisp new gayly flowered curtains brightened up each room. A smattering of furniture and lamps were set in each room, though they would be making their own stamp on the house once they moved in. There was even a new double bed, all made up with a beautiful quilt with matching pillow shams in the bedroom. Someone had obviously enjoyed making a start of getting the little house ready, so lovingly paying attention to these small details.

"Dad," Ben turned toward his future father-in-law. "I can't believe you're doing all this for us," he said as his eyes teared up. Leah's dad reached out and hugged Ben. Then, with his hands on Ben's shoulders, he held him out at arm's length.

"You have made us all so very happy, especially my only daughter. Nothing is too much, Ben."

They got in the car then and headed back for supper. Ben entered the big kitchen, beaming. Leah took one look at him and stopped setting the table to ask,

"What's up with you?"

"I have a surprise for you after supper, is all," was all Ben would commit to.

"Okay," she said, eyeing him suspiciously as she finished the setting the table. Bringing *Oma* to her place in her wheeled office chair, her mom called up the stairs for the others to come to supper.

Four boys hit the stairs running, sounding like a team of horses, laughing and roughhousing all the way down.

"Hi, Ben," they all took turns greeting him, each with a playful slap on the back.

"What's new?" the oldest brother Nathan asked.

"Oh, this and that," he answered, looking at Dad again with a silly grin.

"You're up to something," Leah said, able to read him already.

"Let's pray, then," Dad coughed slightly and interrupted.

After grace, Dad turned to Leah as her mom got up to serve the meal. "Have you heard anymore how that young Amish wife is getting on?"

"Better than she was. My Amish friend Phoebe from school is working with the local doctor to address her depression, and their church is really rallying to help, which we knew they would," Leah explained. "I can't imagine what that would do to me, to anyone, really. So awful. I know everyone is keeping them in prayer."

"Good," he replied. "Ben and I are going to take several cords of slab wood over there later this week, free of course. It's the least we can do."

"Oh, let me know when you're going, Corney. I'll send some meals over with you," Leah's mom said.

"That poor girl," she continued. "Some are given such crosses to bear in this life. It is such a mystery. Hopefully, there will be lots of blessings and consolation in the years to come. I don't know how one would pick up the pieces to move on at all. We must continue to pray for her."

Leah took that in and sat quietly looking down at her plate while the conversation continued circling around the table. The whole situation with the Amish young mother had upset her terribly. She felt so very sorry for her, but felt helpless to do anything. Pray, yes, but couldn't one do more? She thought of her own happiness with their upcoming wedding. Was she entitled to such bliss while Faith was barely finding enough of anything to survive for another day? Was her own joy even right under the circumstances? What if Ben was taken from her a few years from now? Was it even worth falling in love and marrying not knowing how long or short a time you would have together? *This whole life is so very risky. Love is risky. What is that saying...* she thought to herself. *'Better to love and lost than to never love at all?' Was that even right? Do we have prayer simply to put off or quell the doubts when they arise? How do we know what to do? How do we even know?* The doubts could engulf one if you let them, she decided in the end, but not before a simple silent prayer that she sent up, hoping beyond hope it would be heard: *Help my unbelief, Lord...*

CHAPTER 15

Susanna & Levi

Susanna was studying in her room after supper was over in the communal dining room. Levi had followed her back down the hall and was stretched out on the bed by the desk, reading the latest issue of the *American Llama Magazine*.

"It says here that alpaca wool is more valuable than llama's. You can pay up to $20,000 for a pedigree alpaca and up to $10,000 or more for a quality llama. Dang! We only get $600 to $700 per hog after feeding *and* raising it. We need to think about having an alpaca farm. This is the way to go. Listen to this, it says, 'It is one of the fastest growing markets in the U.S.,'" he read.

"Yeah," she replied, still very suspicious. "And just remember back to the year we went absolutely whole hog with Jerusalem artichokes? We thought we'd have the best corner of that market, cures diabetes and all, they said, and we were all out there every night weeding that summer and watering them while being eaten alive by the mosquitos, till way after dark and by fall no one was buying them. All those acres we'd converted. A huge flop in the end. But they had us convinced. When was that? 1982?"

Levi nodded as he continued reading. "I wanna try it. I'll talk to the steward tomorrow."

Their wedding was only weeks away now. Life wouldn't change all that much with Susanna still studying every night until she graduated in June and Levi working with the men on the farms or in the fields six days a week, but they'd have their little home to call their own where they could start a family, joining the cycle that has been running its course from the beginning of Time, always finding young people eager to continue perpetuating God's plan for them, clueless as to what the future might hold for each one.

"Time for you to go home, Mister. We have to be up early," she said as she packed up her books and headed toward the door, but not before they had the chance for a quick hug and an even briefer kiss goodnight.

"Mmm," he hummed. "Any chance for another one of those?" Levi teased.

"Nope," she quickly answered, pushing him toward the doorway. "Pretty soon we'll be married, and you can have all the kisses you want then, sir. Goodnight," she said with another playful push. She closed the door behind him, satisfied that she had tackled enough studying for one night. It was crucial that she not let her personal life, with all its excitement, just now take precedent over school, with it being so close to the last stretch. She'd put in so much time, (and tears) while slogging through some of the more difficult courses, staying up far too late to study for a test whose whole subject matter still evaded her understanding, or an essay that just wasn't coming together, sounding to her more like a fifth-grade report than a college paper discussing the latest research study on adolescent mental health.

March 12

Dear Ivan,

I can't thank you enough for the wonderful visit. Please thank everyone for me. Here we are coming down the home stretch with school. Finally, a light at the end of the tunnel. I got an A on my term paper. What a relief.

Leah and I study together most nights at either her house or mine for our finals. We still have classes and weekly tests and clinicals where we go out to different facilities for hands-on learning. Somehow, it's all coming easier now.

I am sure I told you about the buggy accident in the Amish community where my school pal Phoebe lives. She's been pretty involved in some of the aftermath, helping the family deal with it all. So sad. Please keep them in your prayers. I've been helping my Oma. She had hip surgery and is doing really well for someone in her 90s. She is funny and so grateful for even the littlest things we do for her. I love spending time with her.

My other school buddy, Susanna, has been visiting the burn unit in St. Paul where one of the children from one of their Hutterite colonies is recovering. That was a horrible accident. They were all the way up in northern Minnesota, Graceville, so it is closer for Susanna to visit from near here. Each week she brings home their laundry to do and picks up groceries for their motel suite. They've been camping out that way for months now. The little girl is doing much better. She is only three!

I will write again soon. I can't wait to be with you again. Tell me what you are reading now. I can enjoy it vicariously, at least. I send my love, prayers, and hugs and kisses,

Yours forever,
Hilda

March 14

Dear Hilda,

It is so good to hear from you. I miss you terribly. I can't wait until we can be together always. I don't think I will ever take that for granted.

Here we are busy working when we're not shoveling snow. We are breaking all records for that this year: coldest days in a row, highest drifts, most snow, biggest hail ever, too, and it's still coming in March. I keep busy. Last night there was a blizzard—again—and Klaus, Menno, Dad and I took out the truck and just cruised the back roads around here spending most of the night pulling cars that had spun out from ditches and fields. We had the chains hooked up and found one car after another throughout the night. I wonder if they would have frozen otherwise. You couldn't get through to the police or tow trucks because they were getting so many calls. The visibility was zero, so most stayed in their cars, afraid of getting lost if they tried to walk. Not all had even thought to have some emergency supplies in the car for such eventualities. Not even a shovel or a blanket or extra clothes or snacks or water bottles.

How is school? We could have used you here on Sunday. One of our Mennonite neighbors, Amy, fell on the ice on her back stoop while opening the door. Hit her head and is in the hospital with a traumatic brain injury. Funny thing was she had been shoveling the whole driveway and managed just fine till she got to the back door. She can come home soon but will have months of therapy. She still has two children at home who will be a great help, but she'll need extra people around the house. They don't know yet how much ground she will regain in the end.

I just finished reading Marilynne Robinson's Gilead. I can only agree with her: How can anyone even say, "I don't believe in God"? It is like saying 'I don't believe in gravity, and I'll dedicate the rest of my life to proving it scientifically, by George!' Even if I say, 'I believe in God', I am declaring an oxymoron. Poor gnat! Here I stand, with a mass of wet cells for a brain that have been endowed with consciousness, the ultimate, exquisite miracle of creation, and I dare to dismiss its Maker, dismiss Him of all genius beyond anything I am capable of ever fathoming. Such a mystery. That book will stay with me for a good long time.

Write soon.

With all my love, prayers, and a hug,

Ivan

CHAPTER 16

Faith

Faith's family had, for all intents and purposes, essentially moved into the little farmhouse. Her *mamm* took charge of the house, the washing, the cooking, the cleaning, the garden and the chicken coops besides. When Faith was napping, which was a good part of each day, her *Mamm* took care of the *bobbel.* Her *dat* ran the barn and the milking operation there, making sure the cows were healthy and had plenty of grain, hay, and clean bedding. It was only a week before that the kind doctor had visited and prescribed the medications for Faith, but he reminded her that it might take up to another week to really kick in and for her to feel the effects.

Phoebe continued to stop by after school every day, her driver patiently waiting to see if she would continue on home or wave him off, choosing to stay with Faith that night. Phoebe stuck her head in the bedroom door, seeing that Faith had probably not left the bed for most of the day; still wearing her nightgown, her hairs undone on the pillow. Waving the driver off by the back door, she sat at the table with Faith's mom, who was playing with the baby.

"She hardly talks. I don't know what else I can do. We were hoping that by now she would be getting on a bit more," Faith's *mamm* worried.

"She isn't going to get over this all at once," Phoebe assured her. "It will take time. The meds should be helping more now, and

I am hopeful we'll see a change then very soon. The antidepressant combined with the antianxiety pill should make a big difference. It won't change what's happened, but it will help her be able to start to deal with her feelings and interacting again. We can try a walk outside later today, check on the chickens, start doing some normal activities. She can help you dry the dishes after supper tonight, sweep the porch, hang up clothes. It will all bring her back."

"*Dat* and I spoke to a real estate agent the other day about selling the farm here. It can't help with everything around here reminding her every single day, every hour," Faith's *mamm* said.

Just then, Phoebe turned to see Faith standing in the doorway to the kitchen. She had heard what her *mamm* said. She'd heard everything.

"No. *No!* I don't want to sell the farm. *Our* farm. We built it up from nothing. It's all I have of Noah. I won't get rid of that. This was *our* life. The good times and the bad. No, you can't sell it. I won't let you. No! Do you hear me?" Faith stormed at them, even stamping her foot.

"Oh, sweetheart," her *mamm* said going to her, hoping to hug her daughter, making it all okay.

"No, *Mamm,*" Faith said, pushing her away and stepping back. "I won't sell. We'll make a go of it. We have some savings. I can hire a few boys to help out. I don't want to move from here. This is all I have, what we built together. Don't you see?" Faith shouted as the tears ran down her cheeks.

Phoebe brought the teapot to the table along with teacups, honey, and cream.

"Let's visit here at the table," she coaxed. Faith came and sat down, taking Patience from her *mamm.*

"I didn't know you felt that way, Faith. I am so sorry. I had no idea you'd thought about what to do," her *mamm* confessed.

"Well, I *have* thought about it. I've thought about it a lot. And about a lot of other things, too," Faith said firmly, still frowning as she stirred a spoonful of honey into the peppermint tea. She continued, "It's not all such a muddle now. I am grateful for that. And everyone has been so helpful. I can't imagine people out in the world going through any of this without the support of a whole community. It is a blessing, but I don't want you to think for me, too. I need to figure things out, though some things might take longer than others. I have to try. I *must* try!"

Phoebe and Faith's *mamm* sat speechless. This was a new Faith. Determined, headstrong, almost confident. Her *mamm* slowly began, "Okay... We'll support where you want us to. Just let us know how we can help."

"Oh, I will. Don't you worry," Faith retorted, still frowning. "I'm going to the outhouse. Here, take Patience, Phoebe. Are you staying tonight?"

"I thought I would, if that's okay with you?" Phoebe offered.

"Sure," Faith said as she headed for the back door, practically stomping across the kitchen, barefoot.

Faith had come back to them, to the land of the living. Later that same day, she even asked her parents to pick her and Patience up for church that Sunday. She had already decided she couldn't bear having everyone fawning over her with their platitudes, hugs, and kisses. She would paste on a smile and not talk unless she absolutely had to. Maybe just thank them for the pies and cakes and all, nod and agree with whatever they might say, not committing to anything.

She laid Patience on the bed where she could watch her as she got dressed for church. She would wear black for a year as was tradition, but Patience would more than make up for both of them in her dusty rose-colored dress and matching pinafore.

Addressing the *bobbel,* Faith asked her, "Are we ready then?" as she patted the round little tummy. Then Patience smiled back, her first smile, locking her eyes with her *mamm's.*

"Aw, you little angel! When did you learn to do that? I don't know what I would have done without you, too," Faith said as she scooped her up. Hugging her daughter to her chest, tears came to Faith's eyes once again. "I don't know what I would do without you, my little marshmallow," she said. "I can't be depressed when

I have you, can I? That is why *Gott* gave you to me, eh? To have and to hold, from now on. We can do this, my pumpkin. *Kumm,* now. Your *mammi* and *doddy's* buggy's here...."

On their way to pick up their daughter, they wondered aloud how she could possibly run the farm on her own, with a tiny baby besides.

"Do you think she'll marry again?" Faith's *mamm* asked as the horse clip-clopped along the shoulder of the road at a quick pace.

"Don't you dare start talking about that to her now," Faith's *dat* warned his wife. "The Lord will see to that in the right time. Don't start matchmaking now, promise me," he insisted.

"Okay," she obediently agreed. "I just want her to be happy."

"I know," he said. "But we have to leave this up to *Gott.* Only He can lead her life after all that's happened. All we can do is trust and pray and be there when she needs us, eh?"

"You're right," she replied. "I asked Phoebe and she's excited that my cousin's daughter, Sarabeth, agreed to *kumm* and help Faith around the house, *ya* know, be a *maud* for a while. She'll be here next Saturday from Ohio. She's only seventeen, but she's been a real handful. They are hoping that she'll come around having some responsibility, being away from home for the first time, but in a safe environment."

"That'll be tricky. Keeping an eye on her while being sensitive to Faith's needs. I hope she's up to it," *Dat* said. "I hope Phoebe's up to it, too," he added.

CHAPTER 17
Susanna & Levi

S usanna and Levi were walking hand in hand around the perimeter of the vast farm after communal supper earlier that evening. Their entire courtship had been dictated by her last year in school. She would be graduating in June.

They had only recently been married in early November. The Christmas vacation was taken up visiting family in all the surrounding Hutterite colonies, some as far as a day's drive away. Whatever tiny snatches of time she could eke out were spent researching her term paper, due the day she returned to school. The ministers gave the nod to allow her to have a computer at home during this last year to facilitate her studies. It was for the entire 'hof's benefit that she would be available as a licensed nurse once she graduated.

"We won't know what to do with ourselves once I'm done with school," Susanna commented as they walked along.

"Oh, I can think of lots of things," Levi slyly shot back, laughing. She playfully punched his arm at that comment.

"But we can spend all the time we want visiting or even going away to see people we haven't seen in ages. It will be so much fun, won't it? And I will have a cook week again and have time to mend and sew your clothes and fix up our apartment. I won't know what to do with myself, will I?" she asked.

Levi squeezed her hand as they walked. "I sure hand it to you, working so hard as you have all this time. I bet you didn't have any idea when the ministers brought up the idea of having nurses at home. It's been a long slog, for sure."

"It has. I couldn't have imagined what it would be like, or how much I had to learn. Whew. I don't know if I would have had the courage if I had any inkling before going into it, knowing all that was involved," she pondered. "Your support, just being there in the evenings while I was studying until the wee hours meant the world to me."

"I sure couldn't have done it," he said. "But it's like we hardly know each other now. We have to get to know each other all over again, *ya* know?"

"I know," Susanna said, getting butterflies all over again. She wondered if their love could remain this new forever. She involuntarily shivered at the thought.

"You cold? We could go back," he offered.

"No," she answered, glad he couldn't see her blushing just then. "I'm fine."

They continued walking well past dusk, until the stars were generously spread across the entire sky above them, from horizon to horizon as far as they could see. The farmland where the Hutterites had settled in the Midwest over a century and a half earlier in 1874, was as flat as a pancake, the rich black soil beneath their feet blanketed in new snow, sparkling back like a mirror toward the heavens above.

They passed the orchards and the seemingly endless rows of turkey barns reaching as far as they could see, smelling them before they could see them. Then they walked past the chicken operation with its lights already glaring for the night, duping the chickens into thinking it was perpetual spring, encouraging them to lay more eggs than they normally would in the winter.

They continued on past the hog barns, which they couldn't smell at all, thanks to the Teflon self-cleaning flooring beneath the huge animals that the brothers had invented and patented only a few years earlier.

They walked past the sleeping gardens that would be producing again in a just a few short months, giving all the sisters the job every evening, except on Sundays, of weeding the expansive row upon row—that is every able-bodied sister under the age of forty-five when one was retired from the obligatory tasks in the garden and also the kitchen rota. Girls were also expected to show up as soon as they could walk, practically.

"Come in for a cup of cocoa," Susanna suggested as they neared her parents' house. "We won't stay long," she promised.

"Only if I get a kiss first," Levi said, loitering beneath the cement steps going up to the door. They were the only people out, foolish enough to brave the cold while the more reasonable *leut* were snug in their cozy homes playing board games or just visiting, babies already tucked into bed, grandmothers knitting and *Ol' vetters* sipping little shots of *schnapps* before bedtime. No one saw them wrapped in each other's arms, oblivious to the world around them, so very much in love. No one heard them again promise their love to the other no matter what life might throw at them in the days and years to come. One last kiss and Levi opened the door to find the family there spread out across the living room, some playing games, others reading.

CHAPTER 18

Faith

Faith sat with the women on the backless benches facing the ministers at the Lapps' farm where the Sunday service was being held. *So far, so gut,* she thought. A few well-meaning women had approached her as she arrived in the house, planting a brief kiss on her cheek in greeting. Her mother had scooped up her sleeping baby and was seated next to Faith. No one so far had tried to console her beyond that, which was just fine with her. She didn't look forward to the meal afterward, where there would be more time for that.

The standard *Ausbund* hymn books were stacked at the ends of each row of benches. As the three-hour service dragged on, and the minister whose turn it now was to elaborate on the scripture reading eloquently droned on without notes, instead all from his heart. Faith picked up the hymn book, hoping to find something to read, with the intention of waking herself up before she became any drowsier. After a quick glance at Patience soundly sleeping on her *mammi's* lap, she opened the book. She loved reading the old hymns, some written as far back as the late 1500s. So full of meaning and devotion, written by the early martyrs of the faith and those persecuted in the beginning of their church's history.

That evening she put Patience down for the night and got into bed herself, the last lamp still flickering on the bedside stand. She opened the *Liedersammlung* hymn book at random on her lap. Many Amish families had copies of this book at home. It was often used when the *youngie* got together for singings, containing a more modern offering of English songs than the older *Ausbung* which was written exclusively in high German.

The book fell open to a hymn she had not heard in many years. Reading it, she suddenly felt *Gott's* presence, an otherworldly understanding of what this hymn meant. It was as if He was speaking to her directly, to her alone. Goosebumps ran up her arms as she read the words. So He *did* understand. He did indeed know what she was living through, and He would be by her side always. Never had she known such grace. To understand, to get a tiny glimpse of His workings here on earth was a gift. An undeserved gift; a blessing beyond hoping for. She wanted to hold this moment in her heart forever. Then it would be possible to live again. Then she wouldn't feel the sting of death all around her. She would no longer dread facing another day. She could live in this love, His love, forever. She read it again, though it wasn't easy seeing the words through the tears that freely flowed from her eyes.

And can it be that I should gain
An int'rest in the Savior's blood?
Died He for me, who caused His pain?
For me, who Him to death pursued?
Amazing love! how can it be
That Thou, my God, shouldst die for me?
Amazing love! how can it be
That Thou, my God, shouldst die for me?

'Tis mystery all! The Immortal dies!
Who can explore His strange design?
In vain the firstborn seraph tries
To sound the depths of love Divine!

'Tis mercy all! let earth adore,
Let angel minds inquire no more.
'Tis mercy all! let earth adore,
Let angel minds inquire no more.

He left His Father's throne above,
So free, so infinite His grace;
Emptied Himself of all but love,
And bled for Adam's helpless race:
'Tis mercy all, immense and free;
For, O my God, it found out me.
'Tis mercy all, immense and free;
For, O my God, it found out me.

Long my imprisoned spirit lay
Fast bound in sin and nature's night;
Thine eye diffused a quickening ray,
I woke, the dungeon flamed with light;
My chains fell off, my heart was free,
I rose, went forth, and followed Thee.
My chains fell off, my heart was free,
I rose, went forth, and followed Thee.

No condemnation now I dread;
Jesus, and all in Him, is mine!
Alive in Him, my living Head,
And clothed in righteousness Divine,
Bold I approach the eternal throne,
And claim the crown, through Christ my own.
Bold I approach the eternal throne,
And claim the crown, through Christ my own.*

Faith finally turned down the wick, blew out the lamp, and fell asleep, a deeper sleep than she had known since Noah and the two little girls had died.

She knew this would now be a new time. She felt renewed,

refreshed when Patience awoke hungry the next morning. She lifted the baby from her bassinet by the bed and brought her up next to her to feed her. She would never feel alone again, and He had given her Patience to remind her of that from now on.

*By Charles Wesley

CHAPTER 19
Sarabeth

S arabeth was incorrigible. Amish girls are supposed to be demure, submissive, quiet, and respectful, right? The list goes on: innocent, subservient, docile, meek, dutiful. Their sole duty in life is to serve *Gott*, their families, and their neighbors. To live a godly life. The Bible mapped this out, beginning with the Ten Commandments. The Amish *Ordnung* picked up on the details after that, clearly and sometimes not so clearly instructing those adherents in all things holy. Parents' duties thus require them to mold their children into observant members of this society. Proverbs 22:6 promises, 'Train children in the right way, and when old, they will not stray.' Armed with a clear path to follow, generations of Amish have lived.

All except Sarabeth, it seemed. It appeared she was bound and determined to flout the norm. As in everything. She wore her dresses too tightly fitting. She flirted constantly. She spoke in a loud, belligerent voice, especially when contradicting her parents. Though they had tried to bend this errant branch, she resisted all means of direction. Discipline didn't work, in spite of her parents' consistent and united attempts on that front. They tried from little on to praise her when she complied and ignore the naughty behavior, hoping for a happier child, more willing to please. They showered her along with the other *kinner* with love to no avail. The other children gladly responded, but not her. Year after year, she was the bane of their existence. Concerned family and friends offered their own advice, and the ministers warned the parents repeatedly that they must take this daughter in hand.

The tantrums when she was two were truly terrible. At three she would go stomping outside if she couldn't get her way, her mother having to leave the other children in the house to run after her and bodily carry her back. The time-out chair was a joke. How do you tie down a hysterical four-year-old? By five, *Dat* often had to be called from the barn to assist *Mamm* in the house with the unhappy child. While most children go through the "but why?" stage, Sarabeth continued to challenge everything and her family saw no end to it, even after years of confrontations, patient explanations, and attempts at reasoning with her.

Mamm tried everything, including changing the family's diet, completely ridding the house of sugar and artificial additives and colors. Even after three weeks, they saw no noticeable change. Then *Mamm* finally wrote to *The Budget,* the Amish-Mennonite newspaper that brought news of the Plain world to each other throughout North and South America, asking for any advice from its readers. An appointed scribe in each settlement sends in a weekly column with all the latest news fit to print from their community. All of a sudden, the mailbox was full of cards and letters from people who wrote back with suggestions and encouragement.

"She will outgrow it. Just show love," one wrote. "We had one like that. Just make sure the parents don't argue or disagree in front of the children," another chimed in. "Are you sure you aren't sparing the rod and spoiling the child?" one post card asked. "She is an Indigo child," another wrote. "There's nothing you can do. It's horrible." The mail on the subject finally slowed to a trickle four weeks later. Then one came that had them all laughing: "If you don't want her, we'll take her. Address below (from Mexico!)" In theory, the suggestions should have worked, but theory is often far from actual reality or fact.

When she reached twelve, they sent her to live with her *mammi* and *doddy,* hoping beyond hope that the grandparents could somehow affect a miracle. She had been tasked with helping the old people, a job many young girls dreamed of. When that didn't prove successful, they even resorted to bribery. If she would only listen and respect her parents, be helpful around the house and obedient when asked.

They knew she wanted a pony. Her dresser was filled with plastic ponies of every size and color, even little technicolor ones with bushy technicolor manes and tails she could brush. She had been collecting them since she was three. Loud exclamations of horses neighing could be heard throughout the house still whenever she played with her teams of horses in the room she shared with her two sisters, and then shouts from imaginary riders ordering *Whoa*, and *Gay!*

She had recently been offered the bribe: a pony of her own if she could rein in her waywardness for just a month. She didn't agree immediately. She'd decided to think on this a while. Could she do it? What would she gain? Well, a pony, for one. Could she actually keep her mouth shut and not let the errant words erupt without a second thought? Two days later, she brought up her verdict at breakfast. Yes, she'd try. It lasted all of one day.

She really wanted that pony. Badly. She waited until her mother was alone in the house to breach the subject once again. Her mother was busy fixing dinner. Sarabeth snuck into the kitchen on bare feet and sat at the table. Her mother didn't notice her until she turned away from the wood stove to fetch a spoon in order to test the gravy.

"Oh! I didn't hear you *kumm* in," she said, flustered. *No tornado today?* her *mamm* thought to herself. *Should I hold my breath?*

"*Mamm*," Sarabeth began. "I just don't see why I have to be like everyone else. Like some little pawn on a chessboard. My mind just doesn't think that way. I want to be free to think what I want and do what I want. It doesn't hurt anyone else, and I can't see the problem. Why do we have to be like little faceless *Amische* dolls all lined up in a row? Our cows run free in the pasture all day, our cats in the barn climb and play and chase mice, and the horses frolic all over the place until we hitch them up and trot them to town or church. I just can't see it," she exclaimed, her voice edging up by decibels.

"Well, yes, we could all live like animals, but then what would the country look like?" *Mamm* asked, slipping onto the bench at the table with a mug of coffee. "*Gott* gave us brains so we could live civilized lives. Every generation tries hard to find the perfect balance to be peaceful and joyful and prosper. Some choose to live in the world, spending their lives craving *things* and working mighty hard to get it all. Some decide to serve *Gott* and work out what He requires for us to live that out in harmony." At this point, *Mamm* took a sip of coffee before she went on, letting that sink in.

"He doesn't mean for us to just conform mindlessly, but we aren't the only fish in the sea. We have to get along too. The rules, the *Ordnung,* just help us keep that simple. Sure, you can make it all very complicated and spend a whole lifetime throwing out this rule or that suggestion, but we *Amische* also believe in grace, that *Gott* will give us the faith to believe in this life and then live it joyfully. It's our choice. Those who rally against *Gott* and chase something else often find themselves just as *ferhoodled,* (flummoxed,) wondering which way is better. The grass isn't always greener on the other side of the fence, my dear girl."

Mamm quietly watched as Sarabeth tried to take that all in, all the while praying that something she said would make a connection there.

"Are you up to collecting eggs now?" *Mamm* asked, hoping to give her daughter some time to ponder these things.

"Sure," Sarabeth said, popping up, heading for the mudroom and grabbing the egg basket there. *Mamm* was surprised there was no objection to her request. *Humph. Maybe we are getting somewhere,* she thought to herself. *Dear Lord, give us wisdom...and patience. Please, sweet Jesus.*

CHAPTER 20
Phoebe & Stephen

Phoebe and Stephen were expecting twins sometime in June. No Amish mother will ever tell you the exact due date. The only answer that has ever been given is, "Time will tell...." Ambiguous, yes, but telling others to mind their own business and at the same time literally trusting *Gott* will make it happen at exactly the right time. Phoebe's midwife begged to differ.

"Babies decide when they are 'cooked' and when their birthday will be," Roberta would remind them.

It was a beautiful early March morning. You could almost believe spring was trying to sneak in, with the days now occasionally bringing the warm Chinook winds from the south, though there was still snow on the ground in sheltered places. *Mamm's* side of the house was literally an obstacle course. There were flats of tiny seedlings everywhere, mostly along the baseboards in all the rooms, tucked on windowsills, and any available nook or cranny where they wouldn't get trampled. There were herbs, squash, pumpkin and cucumber seedlings spilling over their containers. Pole beans, and tomatoes. There were Romas for sauces, and four other varieties already six inches tall. As soon as the threat of frost was gone, they would all go in the garden, which was growing bigger every year, even though all the children had flown the nest, all except Phoebe who was living in the *dawdi haus* with Stephen next door. It was a perfect arrangement for them, at least until she graduated from the nursing program at the college.

Her driver, faithful Mr. Schrock, still drove her to school and back every day where she would meet up with the other Plain girls enrolled in the LPN nursing course. "The Four Musketeers" they called themselves. Susanna was from a Hutterite colony, and Hilda and Leah were Mennonite. The Plain communities in Wisconsin had been considering for some time now, sending one or two girls to the program in the hope of helping their young families get good advice at home and maybe avoid numerous doctor visits unless truly warranted. They could also then better help the elderly in their communities and assist those choosing to stay home at the end of their lives.

Today, Phoebe had asked Mr. Schrock to drop her off at the Stoll's farm after school. She had been visiting with Faith and her infant daughter Patience ever since the horrible train accident that took the lives of her husband Noah and their two little girls, Hope and Charity.

Faith had rallied after the accident, though it had taken herculean strength to move forward. The fact that she and her tiny baby, Patience, had not been in the buggy that fateful day, gave her something to live for. She had decided to keep the farm against her parents' advice to sell and move home, and things seemed to be running quite smoothly with the help she had hired.

Only yesterday, the letter had arrived with the offer of a *maud* to help her around the house. The letter explained that she was not to pay the girl at all. It was a gift from the family that understood her hardship, having lost both their house and barn all in one night years ago now, the work of teenage arsonists with nothing better to do on a Saturday night. Luckily, no lives were lost in that fire, but all of their cattle and horses were gone. It would take years to restore what had been lost. The surrounding Amish communities had risen to the occasion back then and saw to the rebuilding until it was completed, all without charging a penny to the family.

Sarabeth was due to arrive in a week on the Greyhound bus.

The letter was signed by the girl's mother. A short P.S. was the only vague indication that the girl might not have been completely in agreement with her new assignment. "She is young and hasn't been away from home to work before, but we insist that she try this," the P.S. stated. Not much to go on. *Well, this can't be too hard,* Faith told herself. She, of course, had no idea what they were in for. Time would tell...

Sarabeth was all of seventeen. She had barely scraped through the eighth grade in school, thinking she knew as much, if not more, than the new teacher who was only three years her senior. It had been Bernadette's first year teaching and the tall, rail-thin girl with her 'attitude' was enough to make her seriously consider giving up teaching all together. But she didn't. She knew that Sarabeth would not be back next term, so Bernadette willed herself not to cry in front of her students and not give up.

Sarabeth's *mamm* was furiously sewing new dresses for her before she'd leave for Wisconsin by the weekend. Sarabeth insisted she didn't need them but *Mamm* had put her foot down saying she did need them and she wasn't letting any child of hers go away in the too-tight and too-short *tracht* she had been hanging onto these last two years. They weren't presentable. They weren't even modest. The battle had raged on all day and into the evening until *Dat* came home and put an end to the rowing.

"You will *only* take your *new* dresses and that is that, Sarabeth," he said, laying down the final word on the matter. "And you will see how you can help the poor *frau* whenever possible. She has been through the wringer, losing her family and all. You will be polite, obedient, and friendly. Lord knows she needs all the friends she can get now."

"You will write to us, won't you?" her *mamm* asked.

"I guess so," was her noncommittal answer.

"You will, missy!" her father insisted, looking up from reading *The Budget*.

"Okay. I'll try. I really will, *Dat*. And *Mamm,* I will let you know how it is. I just hope they let me go to the singings and all..." she began. *Dat* cut her off right there.

"Your first task is to help at home. Don't go off wherever or whenever your whim takes you. You have a job to do. It doesn't end just because there is a party or a singing. You got that?" he demanded.

"Yes, *Dat*," she answered.

"Now try this one on so I can hem it," *Mamm* asked Sarabeth as she handed her the dress she had been hurrying to finish. Taking it upstairs, she soon came back down looking like a new girl.

"It's perfect!" *Mamm* exclaimed.

"Now, that's how you should look," her *dat* added, peering over the top of the newspaper.

She hated to admit it, but the sky-blue dress was beautiful, and it felt so new and pretty.

"*Denke, Mamm,*" she said with a shy smile.

"Now that's three so far. I want to make two more and a couple of aprons for every day and church ones, too. *Kumm* here so I can pin the hem."

Her first thought was to tell *Mamm* not to make them too long in the hem, but she decided against that. *Mamm* knew how to make dresses and the truth was Sarabeth had never even sat down at a sewing machine, preferring to ride the horses bareback in the fields or climb trees or hide on the old tar-papered outhouse roof by the barn where no one would see her reading the latest forbidden paperback she may have shop-lifted from a recent trip to town. *Mamm* had begged her to learn to sew but gave up trying in the end, worn down by the constant contradicting retorts. *Maybe going away will make her more reasonable, Mamm* thought to herself. *Young people often think their lot is the worst possible and rebel, at least until they see how other families struggle under their hardships. At this rate, no one will want to marry her. She can't sew or cook or be agreeable most days. Lord, help us do the right thing for her...*

That night Dat brought down the suitcase from a shelf in their bedroom closet. *Mamm* had even made a pretty zippered toiletry bag and filled it with a new hairbrush, a new toothbrush and various things Sarabeth would need. Then *Mamm* wrapped up several jars of her strawberry jam in newspaper and tucked those into the suitcase as well. They left it open on the sofa and shared mugs of cocoa before their prayers together and then turned in for the night.

CHAPTER 21

Faith

Phoebe, her *Mamm* and Faith sat at the kitchen table. It was well into April, evidenced by the fact that she could now open the windows and freshen up the house during the day. Phoebe had just been dropped off by her driver, Mr. Schrock, after school was over. She could ride home in the buggy when *Dat* came to pick *Mamm* up or she could spend the night, though Faith's *mamm* often came for the night shift.

Faith was doing so much better now, running the farm quite efficiently with the two *boova* she'd hired, brothers from one of the neighboring Amish farms up the road. In spite of being so young—only sixteen and seventeen—the two boys had been trained well. They drove up in their little trap or roadster buggy at five sharp, even in the rain, every morning. They got right to work mucking out the stalls in the barn and laying down fresh bedding, feeding and watering the horses, donkeys, pigs and cows. Next, they milked all the cows and then led them to the pasture for the day.

Faith had only this week decided she could take over the chickens once again, especially with one *frau* or another or her *mamm* still coming to spend the day with her. She hadn't been left alone once since the accident, though she felt like she would do just fine on her own now. She tired of the endless chatter of the women who came who thought they would keep her company.

But then, she could leave Patience with whoever was there that day to work in the chicken coops for a while. Before they left after chores each day, the two young men would pick up the large brown eggs that she'd washed and put into cartons. They would drop them off at the Amish store on their way home where they sold like hotcakes. They would also take the livestock to the auction at the beginning of summer, sparing her the job of arranging their sale. Things were definitely working out. No one thought she could run the farm by herself, but here she was, doing just that.

The heartache was still there. She knew it always would be. She thought often of the children and her dear husband and tried to remember how they looked the last time she had seen them before they left that fateful day, never to return. She had straightened the two little girls' stiff black travelling bonnets and buttoned up their going-to-town sweaters. The children called them their 'library clothes' though they were the same outfits they would wear on church Sundays or for going to the doctor's office, but also the town library on even rarer occasions.

She didn't have a photo of them. Not one. Long ago the Amish had deemed photographs in the same camp as idols, the making of images to worship, which the Bible clearly forbid. She wondered if her memories of them would fade over time but was convinced they would never leave her. Maybe they could even see her from Heaven. Dwelling on these thoughts still made her sad, even turning on the faucet on the tears once more, even though she didn't believe it possible one could cry so much or so often. And letting herself become sad or despondent might even drag her back into that black vortex of depression that she almost didn't survive. Was it only six months ago? She shivered whenever she thought about those months, the darkness, the feelings of despair, of not wanting to even live another day. She could easily have ended up in one of those places for hopeless cases. She marveled that she hadn't. She had read about them, those asylums, though they aren't called that anymore. Just the thought of it made her shiver. Grateful. That's what she could concentrate on now. Being thankful. Even Jesus had gone through the darkest journey anyone could go through. He had felt abandoned, betrayed, certainly He understood her sufferings, and they were nothing compared to His.

No, she couldn't let that happen. Patience needed her and her family had convinced her that they needed her, too. She was lovingly cared for day by day and somewhere along the way had even found forgiveness in her heart for all of her anger and doubt. She would never understand why, why it was her family. Why anything bad ever happens to *gut* people. Why them? She could only acknowledge that us poor souls down here will never understand the divine will of *Gott*—never but try to believe and ask for His help to overcome our unbelief.

Phoebe's *mamm* had written to her cousin in Ohio asking if her daughter, Sarabeth, might be interested in working as a *maud* away from home for a while. *Mamm* was hoping that Faith would welcome a live-in mother's helper, freeing the older *fraus* from taking turns being at the farm so she wouldn't feel lonely or depressed. They were more than willing to help, hoping that the serious depression she experienced in the beginning right after the accident and had lasted for weeks would not return again.

Her cousin, Lovina, had written back a short letter, effusively grateful for the opportunity for her daughter Sarabeth. *Mamm* had heard whisperings about this difficult daughter before, but hoped she was growing out of it, whatever 'it' was. Her cousin certainly didn't elaborate, but just seemed very anxious to farm the girl out. *Mamm* figured they'd just have to see if this scheme would work when she arrived.

Faith thought it was a *gut* idea when *Mamm* explained the plan. She was deeply grateful for everything everyone in the *Amische* settlement had done for her, but she was starting to feel like it should be time for her to stop depending on them all, taking so many away from their own homes and duties there. Sarabeth would be arriving in four days. Faith was excited at the prospect. She could certainly say if it wasn't a good idea after a few days with the girl. Well, time would tell....

Later that day, she heard a horse and cart drive into the farm. The flatbed behind the horse was filled with greenhouse flats of flowers and vegetable seedlings. Before she could settle Patience in her cradle, the sound of a motor was already revving up. She ran out the kitchen door to find her *dat* and her four brothers tilling her garden patch from one end to the other. The little motorized cultivator was cleanly ripping through the rows and had the job done in no time. Then the boys started grabbing boxes off the flatbed and setting them at the end of each row.

"It'll be a full moon tonight, Faith," her eldest brother reminded her. "The second quarter moon started last week, so we have to get these in today," he said as he wrote in marker on the wooden stakes he'd brought along with the name of the vegetable or flower seedlings they had just planted and stuck them in the ground by each row. "The Old Farmers' Almanac never lies," he added.

It was almost dusk, but the boys kept at it until all the little containers were empty and stacked neatly back on the cart.

"You must *kumm* in for supper," *Mamm* insisted.

"Not this time," they answered. "Hazel is holding supper for us," Elmer informed her. "Just make sure to water it all tomorrow early if it doesn't rain tonight," he added.

"Oh, I will," Faith said, hugging each brother as they tried to slip away. "*Denke* so much, you guys." Finally, they were all off.

"Well, what do *ya* know?" Faith marveled as they sat back down at the table for supper.

"My garden is in, the barn is taken care of, and my supper is already made. I could get used to being spoiled like this," she said as she spooned up the piping hot *rivvel* soup and blew on it.

"They say the garden has to be in before the last full moon in May. I always thought it was an old wise tale, myself," *Mamm* stated.

Phoebe set her spoon down. "Um, *Mamm,* I think you meant an old *WIVES'* tale?"

"That's what I said," she insisted, going back to her soup.

"Stop correcting me, missy," *Mamm* said, pointing her soup spoon at her daughter for emphasis. "Now that you're going to college you think you know everything, eh?" *Mamm* frowned and fussed at Phoebe.

Faith laughed. "You two never stop, do *ya?*" Just then they heard Patience fussing in the bedroom. Faith and Phoebe jumped up at the same time to get her. Faith made it in first, scooping up the happy baby. "Whew, you need a change. Should I leave you to your auntie Phoebe then after all?"

"Sure," Phoebe offered.

"No, I was just teasing," Faith said, hoisting the baby up onto her hip and grabbing a Birdseye diaper off the neat stack on the end of the changing table. "You smelled *rivvel* soup, eh?" she asked the baby.

"Ok, I'll let you taste mine," she told the eager *bobbel*.

Settled back at the table with Patience belted into her high-chair, her bib on and her pudgy little arms waving her excitement, Faith blew on a spoonful of the good soup and finally offered it to her. Of course, it was gone in a split second.

"You like that, eh?" Faith asked. "You'd eat anything, I'd wager," she said while she blew on the next spoonful of soup.

"She's a *gut* eater," *Mamm* said. "You won't have to worry about her being the picky one." *Mamm* continued, "We had some neighbors when our first, Abe, was little and their *kinner* were such fussy eaters. He must have been about two or three then. Yes, it was. It was shortly after we had visited them before, so the kids knew each other already. Well, it worked. They invited him over one day and sat him across from their children lined up on the bench at the table at lunch time and the *kinner* just watched him with their mouths open. He just kept eating whatever their *mamm* put in front of him. Soup, sandwich, pudding, he slowly finished it all off. Well, it actually worked. Halfway through the meal, their kids picked up their spoons and followed suit. They kept him for supper too that evening and brought him back later. He sure cured them all!"

Dat showed up then with the buggy just as Phoebe was serving dessert. There were still plenty of desserts showing up at

Faith's house, proof that she hadn't been forgotten, even after all these months. They insisted he sit down and enjoy the lemon sponge pie with them, which he didn't refuse. He had brought Faith's mother who would spend the night, relieving Phoebe and her *mamm*.

In the buggy on the way home, they rode quietly, all pretty much spent from their busy day. Finally, *Dat* cleared his throat.

"I had a visit from Faith's *dat* today," he began. "He'd gotten a letter from some relative of his who is a bishop up in Manitoba, Canada, at that new settlement up there," he explained as both *Mamm* and Phoebe turned to look at him.

"He wanted to know if I thought Faith might be ready to consider marrying again. He knew Phoebe and you, *Mamm*, have been pretty involved with the whole situation these last months."

"But it's hardly been a year, *Dat!*" Phoebe shot back, horrified.

He agreed, "Yes, but they would still want plenty of time to get to know each other and visit maybe, back and forth, *ya* know?"

Mamm asked, "Do you mean the bishop is interested for himself, or does he write for someone in his congregation?"

"There's a widower up there who lost his wife last year. It was cancer. She was only thirty-five. She left six *kinner*," he explained.

"Oh my," Phoebe declared. "It's so far away from her family. I couldn't imagine leaving here if it were me."

"He could always *kumm* this way, *ya* know. They might not even like each other. We'd just have to wait and see. Next time you're at Faith's place, you could bring up the idea," he added. "Sort of tactfully see what she thinks."

"Oh, I just don't know," *Mamm* said, worrying her handkerchief. "I'd say she's still a bit fragile, for all the determination and gumption she puts on."

"But is anyone ever ready after so much heartache?" *Dat* asked.

Phoebe was still shaking her head. "I think it is too soon, *Dat*."

"Okay," he said. "We'll pray on it for a bit, then."

Stephen came in through the mudroom at the back of the house and, kicking off his chore boots, headed for the sink in his stocking feet to wash up, but not before a quick detour to plant a gentle kiss on Phoebe's lips. She was at the table doing the eternal homework assignment.

"How was school today?" he asked.

"Gut. I'll be finished with this in a minute," she said without looking up.

Stephen walked back to the mudroom door and stood in the kitchen doorway quietly waiting.

"What are you—" Phoebe finally turned to look at him. "OH!" she squealed. "You finished it, you sweetheart!" she said, noticing the second cradle he had made. He'd made one when they first found out they were expecting, but then, when they were told they were having twins, he had begun a second cradle. Now it was done, the gleaming, freshly oiled oak lovingly hand crafted.

"It's beautiful, Stephen," she said, attempting to hoist herself up from her chair. It was getting harder each day to maneuver her bulk from one place to the next.

"Let's just hope it isn't triplets," she teased.

"That isn't even funny," he said, frowning. "Please don't bring that one up again. I don't know how we'd survive that. Our *haus* is too little to begin with, Pheebes. I don't know where the second cradle is even going to go yet, much less more furniture."

"I see Roberta again tomorrow," Phoebe finally told him when she had managed to stand up, both hands rubbing her lower back. "I don't know how much longer I can do this. I don't have any room left to even eat! I don't look forward to labor, but I'm about ready to do anything, even that really, just to have this part over."

"Well, remember the midwife said not to rush them; just wait till they're ready. We don't want them *kumming* early and having to keep them in the hospital at all," he reminded Phoebe.

"I know," she agreed, groaning and stretching her arms over

her head. She reached toward him for a hug but soon realized the great bump between them prevented such affection.

"I haven't seen my toes in weeks!" she moaned. He came up behind her instead and wrapped his arms around hugging her that way.

"Just hang in there a bit longer," he coaxed, kissing her shoulder. "I think in a few short weeks we will be walking them around here at night, listening to them wailing and wishing we could have this quiet time back somehow."

"You're right," she admitted. "but I don't expect them to be wailing," she said, turning back around to face him. "Babies only cry when they need something. It's their *only* way to communicate with us or the outside world. There is no reason to let them cry at all. You pick them up and figure out what they want. Either they are cold, or hot, or wet or hungry or just want to be held, which is perfectly valid, too."

"I hope you're right," he said, skeptically. "My *mamm* might not agree with you."

"Oh, our babies won't need to holler," she tried again to convince him. "We had a unit in college on infants and had to read and report on a book on the subject and the book I chose ended up being absolutely fascinating. It was *The Continuum Concept* or something. This fashion model from France went on a fling to South America with two guys she'd just met at a cocktail party of all things, hunting for diamonds and ended up staying while her friends returned. She lived with a primitive indigenous tribe there and documented their bonding behaviors, which had struck her as being so very different from anything she'd ever seen before. She claims in the book that their children didn't fuss like ours do, like babies in first-world countries."

"I'll believe it when I see it," he answered, still skeptical.

The next day was Saturday, and they went to their midwife appointment in town together. After measuring and checking everything, Roberta declared them 'cooked.'

"They can come any time now," she allowed. "They are both head down, both over five pounds by my calculations, and everything looks good. Call me when things start up, okay? I'll meet you at the hospital."

"It's hard to believe this stage will ever end," Phoebe said, shaking her head as she tried to wiggle off the exam table. It took both Stephen and Roberta helping to get her standing upright again.

"Well, believe, my dear," Roberta said. "I've never known any that didn't come out eventually," she added, chuckling.

Steven said then, "If this goes on much longer, I'll have to find two short people to walk in front of you and hold up this bump so you don't fall over forward. I can't believe skin can even stretch this much. It's *ferhoodled!*"

CHAPTER 22

Sarabeth

Her *mamm* made Sarabeth her favorite supper: Showboat casserole. She'd never known why it was called that, but the name had stuck somewhere along the line. It was just spaghetti and meat sauce mixed up well and put into a deep buttered, covered dish to bake for an hour or so. About fifteen minutes before taking it out, two cups of mixed shredded cheese are dumped on top and the heat lowered or turned off and left to melt.

She was leaving later that night on the Greyhound bus. There was only one bus per day going out of the closest town to them in Ohio. *Dat* had arranged for a Mennonite friend who often drove for the Amish to pick her up at 10:00 p.m. She had never been on a trip like this before, or on a coach at all, much less for twenty-four hours. Eastern Ohio was that far from western Wisconsin. At least it was with all the 'milk stops' along the way. That's what *Dat* called them, the tiniest towns still on Greyhound's route.

"Do they stop for bathrooms on the way?" Julie Sue, who was four wanted to know.

"They stop at all the towns on the way, but they tell everyone how much time they've got before the bus has to leave again. They have a tiny bathroom at the back of the bus though," *Dat* explained. "If they are making *gut* time on the road they will stop and change drivers at designated points, usually at a big truck stop with a restaurant where they'll give you a meal break for an hour."

"They don't have any food on the bus?" *Mamm* wanted to know.

"No, but you can bring your own along," *Dat* informed them. Looking directly at Sarabeth, he continued. "You are not to talk to any men or boys on the bus. At all. I mean it. Did you get that?" he added for emphasis.

"Yes, but what if they talk to me first?" Sarabeth wanted to know.

"It doesn't matter. All sorts of people travel by bus, and you can never know what they have on their minds. They could even be downright dangerous. You don't know what they're up to, so you just don't get involved. Your cousin's *dat* will be there to meet you tomorrow. It's all arranged."

"Okay," Sarabeth answered soberly, uneasy for the first time since they'd planned the trip.

"I'll give you enough money for meals along the way, and we'll pack up some fruit and sandwiches. You have Phoebe's address and Faith's, too. I don't expect any problems," he concluded.

Mamm had been sitting thoughtfully and finally spoke. "You know, our dress is a witness to what we believe. Don't flaunt that. It is also a protection. Our *kapp* or bonnet also tells the outside world what we believe and Who we are living for. Act modestly and you will be protected."

"Okay. Now you are making me nervous," Sarabeth said.

"Keep a prayer on your heart at all times and you will be safe," *Dat* added.

"Will there be cowboys on the bus?" Jethro wanted to know. He was six.

"Probably not," *Dat* said, chuckling.

Then Eliza Jane, who was only five asked, "When are you coming home, Sara? I'll miss you," she said tearfully.

"The time will go fast," Sarabeth assured her. "And I'll bring you home a present when I come back."

Eliza Jane furiously clapped her hands then, inadvertently flinging her fork across the kitchen floor with all its contents landing somewhere along the way with a loud splat. No wonder they often called her Calamity Jane.

The van arrived right on time with nine other passengers all destined for the Greyhound station. Two hours later they were dropped off at the border of Holmes and Wayne Counties where the little bus station sat next to a barber shop on one side and a mom-and-pop grocery store on the other side of it, one of only six establishments on Main Street.

Sarabeth was far too excited to sleep. She looked at all the people sleeping on the bus sprawled out in as many different positions as she found an empty seat next to a little old grandma who was wide awake, furiously knitting away.

"Oh, hullo, dearie," she said. "How far are you going?"

"Green Bay, Wisconsin," Sarabeth answered. "And you?"

"Oh, I get off in Minneapolis. It's a long trip, so I'm glad for someone to talk to," she explained. "I've been visiting my grandbabies in Pittsburg and going back home now. They are cute, but they sure do wear you out. I'll need a vacation just to recuperate," she said. She drew out a Tupperware container from her knitting bag. "Cookie?" she offered Sarabeth.

The next stop was in another small town along the route. A large man got on the bus which immediately took off again as he wobbled down the aisle looking for a seat while clutching at the tall seat backs to steady himself as he made his way, passing Sarabeth and the old lady but not before Sarabeth recognized that he was Amish. The hook and eye clasps on his jacket were a dead give-away, as were his broad fall or barn door trousers, a very conservative *Amische* giveaway; maybe even one of the Schwartzentruber Amish from Ohio or Cambria County, Pennsylvania. She soon forgot about him as the woman next to her chatted on and on. Sarabeth found herself nodding off. Sleeping a bit would make the time go by, she thought.

She woke as the bus pulled into a truck stop around 5:00 a.m. The driver turned on the speaker system and announced an hour breakfast stop. It would be good to get up and stretch a bit and have something hot to drink.

The old lady stuck by Sarabeth, which was fine with her. They found a booth and sat down together. A waitress came by a minute later and took their order. While they were waiting, Sarabeth looked out over the vast parking lot from where she was seated. There were trucks parked or idling as far as the eye could see. Then she saw the Amish man waiting by a curb on the service road near the truck lot. A car drove up and stopped in front of him and a woman got out. She carefully walked around the car, her spiked high heels forcing her to practically tiptoe her way there and talked to him for a few minutes before he got into the passenger seat.

That is odd, Sarabeth thought to herself. *That woman looks pretty fancy to me with all those hairs and makeup and those clothes.* The world sure seemed like a strange place to her just then. Dat *must have been right. It could be downright dangerous out here,* she told herself as she watched the car pull away.

CHAPTER 23
The Four Musketeers

The Four Musketeers hadn't seen each other during the holidays and now that break was over they were eager to catch up. They were back at college for the final slog. Licensure board testing would happen at the end of May. Term papers were turned in just before Easter break, so they were looking forward to seeing their grades for that. Lunch time couldn't come fast enough. The morning had been spent reviewing the main parts of the final exams. The class was down to nine from thirty two years ago. It wasn't that the material was so very difficult. Those numbers could be blamed on a whole host of other things. For one, scholars were marked off for failing to show up on clinical days in full uniform. Attendance was crucial. More points off for a no-show. Turning in homework on time was vital. No extensions.

The original class was made up of an assortment of women. Some had dropped out of high school or had small children at home and were hoping to improve their economic situations. Others were wishing to make it in the professional world, having tried the only jobs that were available to them without those credentials. One by one they failed to return to classes as they found even the barest requirements insurmountable with babies at home or rifts in their relationships there. They hadn't even managed to get their homework assignments done on time, with returning after a full day of school and all the demands at home waiting for them besides. A couple of these girls had even approached a few of the more studious students, The Four Musketeers included, with offers to pay for a copy of their daily class notes.

"I want to start with all of our news," Hilda began. The others nodded enthusiastically as they unwrapped their lunches. "We've set a date!" she announced. "We're getting married in August." The girls all squealed with delight, their mouths stuffed with sandwiches they only had a short time left to devour.

"Well, we got married," Leah said as she stood, and theatrically topped Hilda's news with a bow at the table. "We have the dearest little house, too, that Ben's father got us."

"It's your turn, Phoebe," Susanna said, hoping to hear any updates on the twins who were originally due in late June just after graduation.

"Well, my midwife thinks they are 'cooked' and can come any time now, though I am hoping to keep them in these next six weeks and fatten them up a bit more. I really want to avoid any of the premature scenarios with their own complications and developmental delays. I may have to go on bedrest soon if labor threatens too early. If I do, I'll figure out some way to study at home, maybe even take the finals from there, too," she explained.

"Oh, we'll all chip in somehow. There is no way you are going to drop out now, sister," Leah promised.

Phoebe looked at Susanna then, guessing correctly that she had some important news, too. "Isn't there something you are going to tell us, Susanna?" Phoebe pried, making Susanna blush.

"How could you tell?" Susanna demanded quite shocked actually, while frowning at Phoebe. At that Hilda choked on her sandwich while Leah gasped and then snorted coffee into her paper napkin, her eyes wide with astonishment, her eyebrows questioning if she had heard right.

"You really want to know?" Phoebe asked.

"Darn right I do," Susanna shot back, totally taken aback.

"Well, the Seven Up instead of your usual coffee for one. And you've obviously lost a bit of weight—morning sickness I am guessing. No one loses weight over Easter for any other reason. Am I right? And the real clincher is the *melasma*," Phoebe explained while the others looked at each other for some clarity. "It's the darker splotches around your upper lip, nose, cheekbones, and forehead. All the raging hormones cause it. It happened to me," she explained, pointing to her own darker pigment around her mouth. "It usually goes away after the birth."

"I never heard of that," Leah cut in, finally recovered from her shock at the news.

"Me either," Hilda said, wiping her lips with the back of her hand.

"Okay, then," Susanna surrendered. "You got me! But it is only one baby. Maybe around only six weeks to two months along. The morning sickness is getting better. I can't believe you knew just by looking at me," Susanna said, shaking her head.

"Well, you two didn't waste any time," Phoebe added, chuckling. "I hope we have reunions every few months after we graduate. I want to see all these married ladies and their babies." They all agreed they would continue to be best friends after school ended. Just then, the bell rang for the end of the lunch hour. As they filed out of the cafeteria, Leah asked Phoebe for an update on the young widow and her baby.

"They are doing so much better," she informed Leah. "And she has a *maud* coming to help her this week. We don't know much about the girl, but it should be interesting. I'll let you know. Definitely stay tuned."

Bedrest it was. At their next prenatal exam, Roberta and the clinic's doctor she was obligated to include in Phoebe's care felt that it would help all around to keep the twins growing a bit more before their due date. Five weeks early wasn't terrible, but it would be better to pass the thirty-fifth week of gestation when the babies' lungs would be stronger, hopefully avoiding any interventions at all to help them breathe.

Stephen was right on it as soon as they got home from the

appointment. He brought in everything Phoebe would need to study and stay indoors and in bed for as long as possible. He brought in a bedside table he'd found in the woodshop's overflow storage area behind the piles of hay in the barn. *Dat* had made it for his father-in-law when he first moved in with them when he was so unwell. Dusted, washed down, polished, and the little caster wheels oiled, it looked like new.

Levi, Susanna's husband, was still apprenticing with Stephen in the furniture business and drove in every morning anyway, so he could bring books and any handouts for Phoebe from school via Susanna. At lunchtimes at school, the remaining three of the Four Musketeers would sign funny cards and send messages along with the books, hopefully encouraging Phoebe to stay put. Levi could also bring any homework from Phoebe home in the evenings for Susanna to turn in to the teacher the next day.

After serving the men breakfast, *Mamm* brought in a bed tray with little legs on it with breakfast for Phoebe. She had eaten with the men but brought her second cup of decaffeinated coffee along with the tray so she could sit and visit with Phoebe while she ate.

"How do you like the holiday sauce?" *Mamm* asked Phoebe. "Maudie had the recipe in *The Budget* last week. The men sure liked it."

"It's gut," she answered, poking the egg atop the English muffin with her fork. "Uh, *Mamm,* I think it is called *hol-LAND-aise* sauce," she enunciated slowly. "It comes from the French."

"That's what I said, isn't it?" *Mamm* asked. "It's so rude of you to correct me all the time."

"I'm sorry *Mamm.* But don't you want to know how to say it right?"

"No, I don't. Just be grateful I do the cooking around here so you can study," *Mamm* said still frowning.

"Oh, I am, *Mamm.* I wouldn't have been able to finish school if it weren't for you," she said, reaching out to squeeze her *mamm's* hand.

"Okay, then. Finish up. Oh, I forgot to tell you, Levi wanted you to know that Susanna is coming to spend the day here on Saturday."

"Oh, that's great! I would be bored out of my mind just lying around all this time. *Denke* for breakfast," Phoebe said as she handed the tray back to *Mamm*. Phoebe picked up the heavy textbook and opening it to the chapter she was reviewing, laid it back down on her chest and was instantly asleep once again.

CHAPTER 24

Sarabeth

The long journey was finally coming to an end. The bus driver announced over the PA system that they would be in Green Bay, Wisconsin, in less than two hours. Sure enough, there was Phoebe's *dat,* her mother's cousin's husband with the van driver right outside where the busses pulled in, that is unless there was another passenger on the bus that she hadn't noticed that was also being picked up by an Amish man wearing a straw hat and sporting a full salt and pepper beard that reached to his waist.

"Sarabeth!" he called as she came down the steps. "*Gut* to see you. How was your trip?" he asked.

"It was for sure loooong," she complained with a dramatic flourish while rolling her eyes. "And you can't really sleep with people talking and the driver announcing every whistle stop along the way."

"Well, let's get you home and rested up first, *eh?" Dat* offered. "Do you want anything to eat before we head out? It's over an hour to our place by van."

"Um, may I have a hamburger and some fries? Please? The last meal stop was at lunchtime. Mable had plenty of cookies—that's the old lady I sat with—but you can't eat just cookies."

"Sure thing. We'll go into the truck stop here and grab some things for the way home," *Dat* offered.

"Thank you very much." Sarabeth was determined to make at least a decent impression. Otherwise, she was in danger of being sent home before she even started working, she figured.

They settled into the van after *Dat* carried the suitcase over, balancing a coffee in his other hand. "Have we got everything then?" he asked. The driver nodded as he sipped his large coke.

"Yup! I mean... yes, sir," Sarabeth said, catching herself. This wasn't going to be easy, she realized, but she still thought it would be well worth it. *New friends, new boys maybe, singings, keeping house with Faith, maybe even getting to ride some horses. I hope the baby isn't colicky or fussy. That would be a bummer,* she thought to herself. *Super bummer.*

"You'll stay the night with us and catch up on your sleep before we take you over to Faith's farm tomorrow. That way, you'll be ready to jump in and help," *Dat* explained.

They finally arrived home. *Mamm* had stayed up and had a pot of chamomile tea and her famous rhubarb crumble should they want a snack before bed. They couldn't convince the driver to stay for snack and waved him off after *Dat* paid him generously.

Sitting around the table, Sarabeth regaled the family with snippets of everything she saw on the trip, including the mysterious Amish man. *Dat* and *Mamm* both looked down, their hands in their laps, shaking their heads at that. Finally, *Dat* spoke. "The devil sure has his ways, *eh?*" though Sarabeth still didn't understand what it all meant.

"I smelled the *wunderbar* snack," Phoebe said as she shuffled into the kitchen from the *dawdi haus* in her homemade slippers and pulled up a chair. *Mamm* reached over and cut another square of the crumble and passed it to Phoebe. Stephen introduced them.

"This is my wife, Phoebe. I'm Stephen, and I can tell you've noticed the twins, too," he said chuckling. Sarabeth's eyes had grown as big as saucers since Phoebe came into the kitchen and slowly sat down, pulling her robe around her girth, though it no longer reached fully across.

"Oh, wow," was all Sarabeth could squeak.

Finally, after the family prayed, with everyone in bed, *Mamm* turned toward *Dat* and whispered, "Well, she seems nice enough. A little young, but it'll be *gut* for her, *eh?*"

"Pretty naïve, I'm guessing. We'll keep an eye on her and check in with Faith to make sure it's all going okay," he answered as he reached his arm over, laying it on her shoulder with an affectionate squeeze.

"Mm," *Mamm* said as she kissed him goodnight, returning the hug. Then she added, "Just remind me not to send any of our *kinner* on a bus trip alone. How scary!"

CHAPTER 25

Leah & Ben

Leah was studying at the kitchen table that morning. Breakfast over, she turned to the necessary homework, even though there wasn't class today, but some kind of teacher's meeting or other.

The day had dawned foggy and cold, the frost pressing itself against the kitchen windows. Leah sat in her usual place with the kitchen's electric light hanging above her, casting a glow on the top of her head, and then making a shadow onto the book.

Ben sat at the opposite end of the table, just outside the small zone of light. They most likely wouldn't work in the garden today. May in Wisconsin was often like this, but it wouldn't last long. The garden needed weeding, but there would be time for that. Ben would be picked up by his father-in-law in another hour as the two did every morning since they went to work together. The lumber business Leah's dad owned was doing well, so well it supported five families in their Mennonite district already, with plans to expand.

Leah and Ben were perpetual honeymooners as far as anyone could tell. They were blissfully happy, never being parted if that could be avoided. They could be seen together at the local dry goods store or the fabric store or the hardware store on Saturdays.

They were fixing up the little house together. Neither made

any decisions at all without consulting the other, whether it was curtains or the color of paint.

"What should I make for dinner?" Leah would ask.

"Oh, anything you want, my darling," Ben would answer.

"But what do you *feel* like having? *Fastnachts?*" she would persist.

"I like all the things you make. I would be happy with a bowl of cereal," he would say.

"Ugh, you silly. Not for dinner!" she protested as he came over and hugged her.

"We aren't getting anything done this way," she pointed out, wiggling out of his embrace.

He would putter about the house while she studied or sit down across from her at the kitchen table and read *The Budget* or one of his other papers or magazines.

"Just think. One more month and I will be done with school. I can't believe it's almost over. I never imagined it would be so all-consuming. And here we are, so close to the finish line," Leah marveled. "I might go over to my mom's later today and see how *Oma* is getting on," she informed him.

"Say hi for me," Ben said. "I hardly get out to see your grandma. I like her. She sure was on our side from the beginning. Pretty amazing for an old lady."

"She is. Ahead of her time, I'd say. She's always been a bit of a maverick. Did I tell you about the time some of our older people started visiting the state prisons? No?" Ben shook his head.

"Well, *Oma* had been writing to one woman on death row for years. The woman had a life sentence after they abolished the death penalty. Anyway, she called ahead asking if she could bring in a Bible to read to her. No, they said. She couldn't bring in anything. She asked about a sheet with Christmas songs she could sing to her. Nope, nothing she was told. Then she asked about Christmas cookies. They wouldn't let her bring in anything at all. So *Oma* thought about this. It was almost Christmas that year.

She was told that she'd be assigned a locker where she had to put her coat and purse before she would be allowed in.

"Finally, the day came that she had been cleared for a visit. *Opa* would have to wait in the car in the parking lot. He wasn't on her visiting list. So *Oma* got in. They even had her take off her shoes and bonnet and felt her hair bun, as if she'd smuggle something in there.

"So they are visiting through a Plexiglass window with a few holes in it. She could hardly hear the woman. Then *Oma* announced she was going to sing to Carol. Carol freaked out, looked both ways and saw there weren't any guards immediately outside the visiting area and said she didn't know if that was allowed. So *Oma* said she'd sing until they stopped her. She stood up then, lifted the hem of her long skirt and there was her white slip underneath with all the words of all *Oma's* favorite songs neatly written out with a black marker, but facing her. The songs started by the hem and worked up toward her waist. She sat back down then with the skirt all folded up and sang all the songs facing her on the slip on her lap. When she finished all of those songs, she'd stand up again and shimmy the waist around to the next side and the songs printed out there. It worked perfectly. All Carol could say was that she thought that was pretty brilliant, and rather gutsy, too. It was definitely a first. That was *Oma*.

"They didn't stop *Oma* singing and the guards even let her stay a whole extra hour visiting. The visits were supposed to only be one hour. She still writes to Carol to this day."

"Hm. That's crazy," Ben stated, and resumed scanning the newspaper.

"I have to tell you this other memory of *Oma*, too," Leah said.

She began, "When I was in first grade, *Oma* was helping out at our little school, working in the library. She'd been a teacher back before she had married, so she knew a bit. The mom who had volunteered before her had left the library in an absolute shambles. She didn't have a clue what the card catalogue was for, so she decided to organize the whole library by a color system she'd devised. Honestly, I didn't make this up," Leah said, laughing. "All the blue-covered books went on the shelves on the right. All the red books on the left shelves, and so on. The whole library got sorted that way. If you came in looking for a book, you just had to know the color and then once you were by the right shelves you had to scan every book along all the shelves looking for your title. It was a disaster! Absolute chaos. And what's even worse was that no one had the heart to tell her what was wrong. Well, when that school year was over, *Oma* convinced the principal to let *her* fix the library during the summer and suggested he also find another job for the mom in the new school year, which he did.

"Well, during Advent that year in first grade, leading up to Christmas, our class was fixing up a manger corner in our classroom. The dads had built us a small kind of half barn and a little crib. We had boxes of dress-ups so we could be kings or shepherds and all. There were enough blue kerchiefs that we could have three Marys at once. It was great fun. So we took all our baby dolls from the dolly corner and took turns singing to the doll in the crib, after rearranging the hay we'd hauled in from the school's barn. We had a real barn by the school where we took care of a couple of chickens, a runty pig, a pair of pigmy goats, a rabbit and a bull calf we named Fritz. Oh, by the way, he was butchered the following year, but none of us kids would touch the Fritz burgers or the Fritz steaks after that.

"So one day, while we had one of the dolls in the crib, one of the girls, my friend Felicity said, 'that isn't the Baby 'cause it's a girl.' Then we realized all our dollies had on dresses and pig tails like us. So we told our teacher, Katerina, what we needed was a boy doll to be Baby Jesus. She said we should bring this big plastic doll down to the library and see if *Oma* could somehow fix the situation. So we trundled down there and she took the doll and assured us she would see what she could do.

"When we came the next morning, we found our Baby Jesus in the crib! He had short curly hairs and was wearing a little white angel gown with tiny stars embroidered on it. We were ecstatic! Our teacher suggested we make pictures for *Oma* to thank her, which we spent the entire afternoon doing.

"The day after that, we had brought our dollies out with us to go sledding after lunch and one of the girls said that Baby Jesus really should have a parka like ours to keep him warm, so we went back to the library to see what *Oma* would suggest. Sure enough, next morning there he was in his crib in our classroom zipped up in a little blue parka with a hood, no less.

"And so it went. I thought he should have something on his feet and told *Oma* when I got home that night. I knew he'd have boots or something on the next day and she didn't disappoint us. Then, Marion Zumpe picked him up and marched him down to the library and asked *Oma* if she could find some tiny mittens for him so we could continue to take him outside with us at recess. The next morning, guess what was hanging on the doorknob of our classroom? It was a pair of little knitted mittens. Marion called them 'mi'uns.' She put them on him and ran down to the library with all of us girls in tow. She walked up to the desk, looked at *Oma* kind of sideways a bit and then asked, 'are you magic?' *Oma* laughed and said no, she wasn't magic, but answered that all sorts of miracles do happen at Christmas."

CHAPTER 26

Phoebe

Phoebe was sitting at the kitchen table in *Mamm's* side of the house. She was reviewing the notes from the lecture that day at school that Mr. Schrock delivered daily since the midwife had ordered bed rest. *Dat* would be coming in from the barn soon for supper. Stephen would be most likely hiking across the field from his furniture shop and barn just about now. It was still chilly in the evenings. Many of the crops had been planted and tiny light green shoots could be seen springing up in rows. The vegetable garden was also well on its way. Finally, the last of the dozens of egg cartons had been cleared out of the house. They had been what Phoebe had come to call a 'fall hazard.' Being eight months pregnant with twins obscured her view south beyond her middle, so she couldn't see her feet or even where she should place her next step these last weeks. Only one nightgown was large enough to fit over her girth; the dresses had been opened to the max. Her carpenter husband had offered to design some kind of little wheeled table that could support her in front so she wouldn't topple over forward with the weight of these babies. She didn't find that even funny. She shuffled back to bed.

Mamm started the little seedlings indoors each February in egg cartons. They were strong, robust little plants by the time they were pretty confident there wouldn't be another frost. Each year, *Mamm* added more plants, and each year *Dat* caved into his resolve not to let *Mamm* talk him into adding 'just a few more rows' when he tilled it. It was a lost cause, though it fed them and their boys' families besides when they harvested the ever-growing plot.

April is lambing season. More lambs are born in the early spring than at any other time of year. *Dat* was kept busy. Although he usually didn't actually *do* anything at the births, other than monitor the progress and look out for the rare malpresentations that could result in the death of the ewe and her lamb, he felt reassured being there. Many nights he would sleep in the barn, hoping not to miss any lambs that might need a bit of help. Twin lambs were not uncommon. He'd even had a couple of triplets over the years. It never ceased to amaze him that after only about four and a half month's gestation, compared to the long nine months' wait in humans, out pops a lamb that can walk minutes after being born and appear fully mature. *Gott's* wonders never cease. The biggest problem was when the ewe appeared overwhelmed and chose to suckle only one of a litter; some checked out completely and didn't nurse even the one. The remaining baby sheep that she apparently rejected needed to be dried and warmed right after birth and then fed with a bottle. If a ewe delivered a stillborn or premature lamb that didn't make it, she might, potentially, nurse one of the rejected babies from another ewe, thus saving the farmer weeks of bottle feeding a lamb.

Stephen looked into the barn after he passed the last field. *Dat* was just finishing up his chores. The six cows had already been milked for the evening and the buckets sanitized and ready for the morning.

"Any more lambs today?" Stephen inquired.

"Two singletons," Dat reported adding, "both tups, rams. Fine black specimens."

"*Gut.* Ready for supper?" Stephen asked.

"*Ya.* I'm ready for sure," *Dat* agreed.

The house smelled wonderful as they came in through the mudroom, kicking off their boots by the door. They hung their straw hats on the high wall pegs as they entered the kitchen, leaving their padded vests there as well before heading for the sink where they could wash up. The single globe lamp directly above the kitchen table sent out a warm glow over the room. *Mamm* was dishing up large bowls of soup from the wood stove and passing them to Phoebe who placed them around the table. Fresh hot Southern Gal Biscuits were in a large bowl on the table next to a block of butter *Mamm* had churned that morning. A very old Amish recipe, the name has been lost to history, but among all the guesses as to its origin, some think an Amish family from some southern state was traveling north with the biscuits to a wedding or such and it got named then.

"Smells mighty *gut,*" Stephen said, turning toward *Mamm* as he dried his hands.

"I know you both like cabbage chowder," *Mamm* answered. "And it doesn't have green peppers in it," she added.

Phoebe groaned. "*Mamm,* you should just cook how you like. He will eat anything. I promise."

"*Kumm,* sit down," *Mamm* invited the men. "I can spoil my only son-in-law a little if I want to," she added. "He's a keeper, *ya* know," *Mamm* countered. "Phoebe, please clear away the rest of all these books and papers," she said.

"We're studying a unit about genetic disorders. It is fascinating," she said as she gathered up her homework from the table. "They are finding that descendants from Eastern Europeans, including the Amish, carry unique traits not found in any other groups. They are hoping to be able to treat these things in children soon, as they discover more about it," Phoebe explained.

Dat thought a moment and then asked, "That clinic in Pittsburg treats Amish *kinner* don't they?"

"That's right," Phoebe agreed. "I cannot imagine having children with those problems. It just breaks your heart."

"*Gott* only sends what we can carry," *Mamm* reminded them. "And special children bring part of heaven with them when they *kumm,*" she added, nodding. "My little sister, Pru, was the happiest child I've ever seen. She was only with us those ten years, but I don't think she ever cried. Sometimes she would look up into the corner of a room from her crib and just laugh and laugh. We used to wonder if she could see the angels. I think she must have."

"Well, let's pray now," *Dat* suggested as he bent his head.

"Mmmm," Phoebe hummed as she took a biscuit from the basket. "I love your Southern Gal Biscuits, *Mamm*. Please pass the apple butter."

They ate and visited over the leisurely supper. When they thought they were done, *Mamm* brought a pie from the pantry to the table.

Surprised, *Dat* asked, "Since when do we have dessert every day of the week now?"

"Since we have two grandbabies to fatten up, that's when," *Mamm* stated as she cut and passed out the vanilla tart, but not before topping each thick wedge with her canned strawberry sauce and fresh whipped cream. "It's a new recipe from Maudie in *The Budget* I've been wanting to try."

"What I do know is that I'm the one putting on weight since you've been pushing the calories on Phoebe!" Stephen chuckled. *Dat* nodded in agreement as he dug into the warm tart, unable to resist it.

When supper was finally over, *Mamm* turned to Phoebe who was helping to clear the table.

"No, no, you. Now I can clean up. Back to bed with you. I mean it. Only three weeks left. You can do it. Let's just get them plumped up a bit more, okay?" *Mamm* asked.

"It's just so boring!" Phoebe whined, setting down the coffee mugs she had gathered up.

"You'll be wishing you could put them back inside in a month or two from now when you're walking the floors with them all night," *Mamm* warned. "Enjoy the quiet now."

"Yes, mother," Phoebe groaned sarcastically, then visibly perked up as she remembered Susanna was visiting her the next day.

"You remember Susanna, don't you, *Mamm?* Tomorrow will be such fun. I can hardly wait."

"For sure, I do. I still can't understand all the colors and prints the Hutterites choose for their *tract*. It's modest for certain, but so... so... loud, *ya* know? Fancy? Orange flowers and red plaids and all. I remember meeting her folks for the first time at the college open school thing. Remember how nervous we all were? It was a bit overwhelming, *eh?*"

"You didn't see the little girls' dresses when we went to visit the colony that weekend. They were even more decorative. Perhaps such a regimented life leaves little for the imagination and the wild patterns just evolved to change up the monotony or such. I know what you mean, though," Phoebe said. "But... *Mamm*.... It was called an open *house* night."

"Just stop correcting me for once, miss high-and-mighty-and-all-educated now, yous!"

"I'm sorry, *Mamm*. It just grates on me like chalk on a black-board. Do *ya* know, *Grossmammi* does the same thing?" Phoebe asked.

"And you set her straight too, *ya? That* is just plain disrespect-ful, now. I better not ever hear that," *Mamm* said, shaking a soapy teaspoon at Phoebe from the sink.

Eager to change the subject she began, "And I still can't believe Ben's *mamm* and sister Emily visited me yesterday. Can you believe it? For almost a year she blamed me for introducing Ben to Leah, and then accused Leah of cradle snatching, as if her little boy had no say in them getting married. She didn't outright ask forgiveness, but she came and sat in the rocker in my room and we had the nicest visit. And she brought that heavenly cherry angel food cake, too. That was a miracle for sure. I thought she was beyond help in the beginning, but she has really mellowed, Praise *Gott!*"

"Well, enough people were praying for her, that's for sure," *Mamm* added. "I didn't think it would ever be resolved, but now look. That is one happy couple, *Gott* bless them. Miracles do happen for certain, dear."

CHAPTER 27

Phoebe

Dat and Stephen had retired to the living room, each taking up a section of *The Budget* that had just arrived that day. All of a sudden, as Phoebe shuffled her way in her floppy pink and purple slippers that her grandmother had made for her, through the house on her way to the *dawdi haus* where she and Stephen lived, *Dat* let out a huge guffaw, making her jump.

"Ach, listen to this one!" he called out.

"I'm right here, *Dat*. You don't need to yell."

Phoebe cut short the trek to her bedroom and sat down on the closest chair to listen as *Dat* read.

"This is from a Mennonite church in Kentucky: 'This older couple were not doing so well, so a young family went to visit them. As they came into the house, they heard a scratchy 'hello.' They didn't see anyone around, but then they spied the parrot. They went into the bedroom and heard the bird again saying, 'it's time to get up.' The dad told them all about the parrot and how he says every afternoon, 'Daddy, did you feed my birds outside on the feeder?' They visited and helped the couple around the house and as they were getting ready to leave, they heard the parrot holler, 'Pray for David and Rosa.'"

"That's a good one," Phoebe laughed. "Is it true?"

"*Ya,* they sent it in. Apparently, it's true. Here's another one," *Dat* said as he turned the page and shook out the paper.

"This one's from Michigan. It says, '... after this young couple bought the house and cleaned it and moved in, they went to make supper. She turned on the gas stove and pretty soon they smelled this awful odor. It took them a while to track it down, but they finally did. They pulled out the broiler and found a roasted rat there.' Ugh!"

Groans could be heard from the kitchen as *Mamm* had been listening too.

"On that note, I will say goodnight," Phoebe said as she resumed her shuffle toward the *dawdi haus.*

"I have a big day tomorrow," she announced to no one in particular. "Susanna is visiting here for the day. I can't wait," she trailed off, closing the door behind her.

The next day blew in with the Spring Chinook winds. Tulips and crocuses pushed up through still-frosty dirt in flower beds around the outside of the house. The sun would soon burn away the lacy crispness covering the gardens without hurting the determined seedlings lined up in rows there. The corn field ignored the frozen dew and raced to meet the sun, growing by inches daily. Birds could be heard heralding the new day, and squirrels were already playing chase up and down the maples surrounding the house.

Mamm and Phoebe sat on the porch wrapped in their woolen shawls, sipping their first coffee while taking in the wonder of a new day. Phoebe was still in her white flannel nightgown, the only item of clothing she owned that still fit her. Everything else had been let out as far as possible and still didn't fit.

"Every night we ask ourselves if tonight will be the night," Phoebe said to *Mamm,* "and each morning we wake up thinking it's never going to happen."

"It will. Just wait a little more," *Mamm* promised. "Your *gross-*

mammi always said you should visit someone and that will bring it on. Susanna is *kumming* today?"

"Yes, she is. Levi is working with Stephen in the furniture barn today so he can drive her. That will be *gut* fun," Phoebe replied.

Just then, Levi's van drove up. Susanna was jumping out before the car had even stopped.

"It's been ages!" she complained as she hugged Phoebe.

"Only two weeks," Phoebe corrected her. "But it seems like forever, doesn't it?"

"Now back to bed, you," Susanna ordered, taking Phoebe's hand and tugging her along.

"So you've come to boss me around today, have you?" Phoebe half-joked.

Settled back in the bedroom, Susanna threw back the curtains and opened a window.

"I brought you something," she announced, producing a gift from her satchel and handed it to Phoebe who immediately started opening it.

"Awwwww," Phoebe slowly breathed out as she lay the gifts on the bed.

"I finally finished them," Susanna said. There were two little knit sweaters, two knitted bonnets and one pair of booties. Susanna had made the first set originally when she first heard that Phoebe was expecting. One set was yellow and the other green.

"They are so darling! Oh, thank you, Susanna," she said tearing up. She wiped her eyes on her nightie sleeve as she wiggled up further in the bed.

"Well, that's the good news, there. Are you ready for the bad, then?" Susanna asked, settling herself on the end of the bed.

"Might as well," Phoebe said. Susanna hauled the satchel up on the bed.

"These are my notes from last week. These are the pretest questions and here are the handouts for our clinicals in the hospital this coming week. It won't take you long."

"Why don't I give you my homework now, so we don't forget it later," Phoebe offered as she rummaged through the papers piled high on the bedside tray-table. "Can you turn it in for me on Monday?"

"Sure thing," Susanna replied.

"I went to see the girl in the burn unit, Ida, you remember her, I think," Susanna began. "She is still in the hospital. It's going to be a long road. It's horrible, but we finally got the ministers to agree to bring in some experts and put together a proper safety program and train some of our parents so we can avoid these tragedies in the future. Only last week we heard that at a *'hof* up in Canada, a mom was trying to cut a chunk of meat with a meat clever in the kitchen while it was still frozen, and it slipped and stabbed her in her middle and she bled to death before the ambulance could get there. No one knew how to cut off the bleeding with compression. She had seven kids."

"I can't imagine. That poor *mamm,*" Phoebe groaned.

"I visited with the little girl awhile and then went to the motel where the parents are still camping out after all these months. I couldn't believe it, though. Liz was sitting on the bed nursing a baby while this other woman was also there nursing another baby."

Liz laughed and explained that this midwife that they knew from years ago up near their *'hof* had come to visit.

"She lives close to the hospital. She and her husband have been visiting Sam and Liz since the accident and have been bringing the babies along—their twins—who are six months old now, the same age as Liz's Daniel. He's still back at the *'hof* and she hasn't seen him in all this time. They wouldn't be able to bring him into the hospital, anyway. As soon as they brought the twins into the room, the first time they came to the motel, Liz's milk let down and she started crying, missing her baby so much. So this midwife-friend, Cora, handed her one of the twins to nurse. The baby didn't seem to care and latched on. It will keep her milk supply up so she can nurse again when they finally get to go home and she can feed Daniel again."

"I wouldn't have thought of that. I guess that works, doesn't it?" Phoebe wondered.

At that very moment, they both heard a loud 'POP.' Phoebe

looked up at Susanna, shock registering on her face immediately. Phoebe froze in place as she frowned, wondering what was going on.

"My water just broke! I can't believe it. Susanna! Oh, help!" she shouted.

"I heard that too. I never knew you could hear it," Susanna said, panic raising her eyebrows along with her voice.

"*Gut* thing I have the bed covered in plastic," Phoebe said as she sat still frozen in place, unable to think what to do next.

"Levi put his cell phone into my purse this morning. We better call your midwife... and the hospital..." Susanna said, making an attempt at taking charge of the situation, but becoming unglued just the same.

Phoebe looked at Susanna. "Better get *Mamm* in here. Then you make the calls. The phone numbers are on a slip taped to my suitcase under the bed. It's already to go. Shouldn't I wait until I have contractions, though? Don't you time them and go in when they're three minutes apart or something?"

"Not with twins. No. We go in *now!*" Susanna ordered, jumping up and falling on her knees on the bedside rug in order to pull the suitcase out from under the bed.

"Okay. Let me use the commode first. It's over there behind the closet curtain. Then you get *Mamm*. Oh, Susanna, I wanted you to *kumm* to my birth so much, but I couldn't think how you could get there with school and all and now you can. Oh, I'm so excited! I'm so scared!"

"You planned this, I bet," Susanna teased.

"No, I promise. I had no idea, really, I swear. It's three weeks early. Will they be okay?" Phoebe said.

"Okay, just don't swear. They'll be good, more than good. Trust me," Susanna said as she helped her friend up and out of the bed and onto the commode.

"You mean this might be my last day being pregnant?" Phoebe marveled.

"You got it...until next time, at least," Susanna laughed.

"Oh, I don't know about that. I don't want to go through all this again, Susanna," Phoebe said, shaking her head, while frowning furiously.

"They all say that. Just wait till you see those darling babies and you'll be wanting to make a bunch more right away. I know a woman who had two sets of twins," Susanna teased.

"I don't believe that. Now just make the calls, okay?" Phoebe said as she positioned her bulk onto the little portable aluminum commode. "I'm afraid I'm going to break this thing one of these times. Is there a weight limit on it? I bet we threw out the paperwork..." Phoebe complained.

"Oh, but she did. Anastasia just had twins, though a couple of singletons are in there, too, I think. I can't imagine all the work!" Susanna said, opening her purse to find the phone and arranging the slip of paper next to her on the bed. "Oh, I'll tell your mom first," she added, jumping up again and going into the big house through the door from Phoebe's bedroom.

"You better come," Susanna said, as she found Phoebe's mother in the kitchen.

"Her water just broke. We better head in," Susanna informed her.

"Oh, my. *Oh my*! Really? Ach, I'll get ready..." *Mamm* broke off as she ran up the stairs, soon running back down with her purse and shawl. Then *Mamm* ran to the barn to get *Dat*, at least as fast as she could manage to run. Then she ran back to the house, completely out of breath by now. She ran to the *doddy haus* to see if there were any new developments. Susanna and Phoebe stood there ready to go, Susanna holding the suitcase that had been waiting under the bed for this moment to arrive.

"Sit down, *Mamm*," Phoebe said. "Nothing is happening. We'll have time. Mr. Schrock will be here soon." Just then, *Dat* ran into the house, also panting. He washed up and then waited at the kitchen door for the car to arrive. Stephen ran into the kitchen next, not sure what all the commotion was about.

"Is-is it really happening?" he stuttered. "R-really?" He was as pale as a sheet, looking from Phoebe to Susanna to *Mamm*.

"Yes, it is," Phoebe laughed. "We have time. Wash up and change maybe. The car will be here soon."

CHAPTER 28

Sarabeth

S arabeth was quite settled in after the first week at Faith's house. They got along well, though it was all so new to Sarabeth. Faith lined up jobs for her to do every morning at breakfast. It wasn't like being at home with *Mamm* at all who would just holler orders all day long as she thought of things that needed doing. It would drag on from morning till night, *enough to make anyone crazy,* Sarabeth thought to herself.

Faith's way of organizing the day didn't seem like having the same pressure. Sarabeth knew what was needed and could take her time. She could ask Faith anything along the way. Faith was still young, as far as Sarabeth was concerned. *Mamm* was already an old *grossmammi.* Maybe that was the difference. *Dat* wasn't around here to bark orders at her, either. She felt freer, somehow, able to spend more time by herself as long as she kept helping. Faith never checked up on her when she was cooking or doing the laundry. She only explained everything first and then just left it to Sarabeth, like she really trusted her. That was a *gut* feeling.

Well before supper each day, Sarabeth would watch the baby while Faith collected the eggs. If it was a particularly nice day, Faith would put Patience in a laundry basket and park it between the clothes lines while Sarabeth unclipped the dry clothes and Faith collected eggs and closed up the chicken coop for the night. Patience would kick her chubby legs and coo as if trying to sing along with Sarabeth while she worked. The *bobbel* wasn't a fussy baby at all, which was a huge relief to Sarabeth. But now that Saturday had come, she was trying to think up a way to ask Faith if she could go to the singing in their district the next night. *Dat* had told her not to even think about it, just to do her job. But there might be some really nice *boova,* she thought to herself. *I might even find my husband while I am here,* she continued to dream. Surely *Gott* already had the perfect mate in mind. He would whisk her away from home to the life of her dreams. It was just up to her to find him, and she didn't want to waste even one singing while on her mission.

The wire egg basket deposited back in the mudroom off the kitchen, ready to wash, Faith headed back out to the yard to fetch her baby. Sarabeth hoisted the dry laundry onto her hip in the other basket and together they went into the house. Faith had started the soup they would have for supper earlier and it sat simmering on the back of the stove, the wonderful aroma permeating the house. The batter for apple fritters was ready to fry.

"Oh, let me make those. I know how," Sarabeth insisted when Faith put the pan of oil on the stove to heat. Faith was pretty sure that Sarabeth really didn't know how to make fritters after several disasters and near disasters she had encountered in the kitchen over the past week, each time prefaced with Sarabeth's assurances that she knew what she was doing. Faith was ready today with her most tactful response yet.

"Well, I learned these from my *mamm,*" Faith began, "and she makes them a little different from most people. Let me show you just one or two," she said as she muscled her way closer to the stove, actually convincing Sarabeth that she should watch. She was trying so hard to butter up Faith before she popped the delicate question about going to the singing.

Faith placed Patience in her highchair and secured her with one of her late husband's suspenders that she had altered for that purpose. Noah had died more than six months earlier when his horse and buggy were crossing the railroad tracks on the edge of town at a blind corner after a morning of running errands and shopping in town. Both their little daughters, Hope and Charity, had also died in the crash. Faith had been at home that fateful day with her tiny baby Patience.

It had been a long hard road for certain, which Faith was convinced she would definitely not have survived were it not for her *Amische* community and the way they surrounded her. No one person possessed the wherewithal to come through such hardship, but they had fought mightily for her, through the crippling depression, through her lack of faith, even supporting her when she expressed her wish to keep the farm she and Noah has built, through it all.

Day and night, non-stop, she was brought into the embrace at the center of the little fold. A very lost little sheep they refused to leave behind. It was still all a mystery to her. Why? Why her family? And then, why are all these people who aren't even related to her giving up their own time and money to be with her and make the farm work? Why was Patience spared, her beautiful precious baby who gave her a reason to live when she had despaired so? It was all too great to understand. *Gott's* ways were for sure too deep and wide for our poor souls' understanding.

The piping hot chicken-corn chowder thickened with Saltines was just the thing for the chilly April evening. For dessert, they would see if they could make a dent in the Shoo-fly pie that had arrived just that morning.

As Faith cut into the sticky sweet pie, Sarabeth took her chance.

"I was wondering if maybe I could, *ya* know, go to the *youngie* singing, like…um…tomorrow night? I am seventeen and don't, *ya* know, wanna miss, like, um, my *rumschpringe*?" she nervously asked, then quickly held her breath, her raised eyebrows hopeful. Amish youth regarded *rumschpringe* as their inherent right. She hoped beyond hope that Faith would not only allow it but perhaps even encourage it. There was a boyfriend out there for sure, if not a husband, Sarabeth was convinced.

When Amish youth reach their sixteenth birthday, they enter into that rite of passage called *rumschpringe*. It literally means 'running around.' The wisdom behind it, originally at least, was that before they join church with a vow of life-long membership, teenagers be given time to see what their other more worldly options in life might be.

This running around usually consists of the young people gathering in a barn on a Saturday or Sunday evening for singing, snacks, board games and such. It gives them the opportunity to meet young people from other districts. Of course, like everything else, some have abused the privilege and drinking parties, and even experimenting with drugs and driving cars (that are hidden later under haystacks) do occur. Most parents hope, at least, that they've instilled good values into their children and can trust them not to throw caution to the wind and end up regretting their choices during *rumschpringe*.

"Sure," Faith said, sitting down and cutting into the pie. She fed Patience a tiny piece, which the baby quickly tongued around her mouth as her arms waved and her pudgy feet kicked the chair, expressing her delight at the gooey stuff.

"You should ride along with the barn *boova* when they leave tomorrow afternoon," Faith continued. "I am sure they will drive you home afterward, too. It would be fun. You don't need to be stuck here the whole time. I'm hardly *gut* company after you've worked all week. You'll have a *gut* time."

You don't know the half of it, Sarabeth thought to herself, the first hurdle cleared. The fact was that her parents had forbidden her attending the singings back home until her attitude changed to their liking. This would be her very first singing. *Maybe they even still practice bundling here,* she slyly thought to herself. *This is getting even better.*

151

Another age-old custom that is now dying out in many Amish settlements is that of bundling. The practice consisted of sleeping fully clothed with another person, as a means to get to talk together privately during courtship. A boy would arrange with a girl what night they should meet. She would leave the back door open and wait in her bedroom fully clothed. He would sneak into the house after he saw the last lantern light extinguished from his hiding place behind a parked buggy in the yard and meet her upstairs. A bundling board about two feet high and spanning the length of the bed is placed between them, obviously with the intention of limiting any romantic contact, though it occasionally failed to restrict such behavior. The purpose was for each to get to know the other and decide if they were a possible contender in the search for a spouse. If they were, he was invited to bundle again until they announced their engagement. If not, the boy was quickly replaced by another eligible suitor.

The day couldn't go by fast enough. Finally, at four o'clock, Faith suggested Sarabeth bathe in the *kesslehaus* and get ready for the big night. Sarabeth had put the largest blue speckled enamel canning kettle on the woodstove there hours earlier for her bath. Pouring the steaming water into the tub, she opened the gravity-fed cold tap, swishing the water with her hand until it was just right. She was glad for the lavender soap her *mamm* had snuck into the toiletry bag before she left. The last thing she wanted to smell like tonight was a chicken coup or dirty diapers. On a trip into town with Faith two days earlier to do some shopping she used her leftover bus money to buy deodorant, a can of hair spray, and a spritzer of cologne when Faith was at the other end of the store. Although not expressly banned, such luxuries were considered outright vanity, worldly, and a waste of hard-earned money.

Right at five she was ready. Faith grudgingly approved of the end results, deciding that a few stray *schtruvvels*, the ringlets obviously very carefully positioned at her temples on both sides and sprayed into submission, outside of Sarabeth's *kapp*, weren't exactly worth insisting on correcting. She had been young herself only a few years ago. What did surprise her was the smell of perfume as Sarabeth turned to go. *I guess you've got to pick your battles,* Faith said to herself as she waved the girl off. *Dear Gott, please protect her tonight,* she prayed.

The two boys and Sarabeth visited on the way to the singing. When they arrived, Sarabeth was speechless. There were dozens of buggies pulling into the field by the barn, boys unhitching horses and leading them to the paddocks and water troughs, lining up the buggies side by side, but not before chalking the owner's initials on the footrest by the dashboard. All were black or regulation gray, though some boasted blinking battery-fueled lights, fancy chrome hardware or brass studded halters, only over-looked by the parents because of *rumschpringe.* They remembered their own running around time and allowed this freedom to the young people, basically turning a blind eye to the shenanigans, praying mightily that their children wouldn't choose to go down the wrong path.

Girls were carrying covered dishes to the house for the snacks and supper that would be served later. Sarabeth followed the two boys in and sat opposite them at what was obviously the girls' side at one of the long tables spanning the length of the barn. Bowls of popcorn balls, chips, dips, cookies, bars and bottles of soda were placed in the center of each table along with *Ausbund* hymn books. As Sarabeth was looking around, unaware her mouth was open and her eyebrows were as high as they'd go, she scanned the steady stream of young people coming into the barn. All of a sudden, a herd of *boova* jumped onto the bench opposite her, displacing the two younger boys and jostling the table as they pushed in, not unlike young stallions.

"Hi there, I'm Ezra..." the tall blonde one began.

His friend cut in, "You're new here..." He had beautiful, dark curly hairs escaping out from under his straw hat. The third one, who had ginger-colored hairs and was shorter than the other two spoke next. "Welcome. Where're you from? I'm Josiah," he said, extending his hand.

"Whoa there, ponies," a girl sitting next to Sarabeth said. "I'm Gertie, and you can ignore these jokers if you know what's *gut* for you," she added sternly, glowering at them.

"Um, well, ah... I'm Sarabeth... from Ohio. I'm the *maud* for the *frau* that lost her family in the train accident." They all nodded, their eyebrows suddenly frowning in appropriate sobriety at the mention of that tragedy. The singing began just then in high German with an old hymn. The songs would progressively become more contemporary and in English as the evening progressed.

Sarabeth slowly sized up each one of the delightful specimens across from her as she mouthed the words, her mind miles from the lyrics, her heart jumping as she imagined running her fingers through that mop of shiny dark brown curls or wrapping her arms around the broad shoulders below the straight blonde bowl cut and blue eyes. The red head was pretty cute, too, if not harder to read. Mysterious even. *But those curls! Swarthy. Yes, that's what he is,* she told herself, remembering the word from a western romance novella she had shoplifted from the drugstore just the month before. *Oh, drat it all!* she thought to herself. She had left that book under a loose shingle on the outhouse roof back home. *It'll be a soggy mess by now. Oh well. Can't be helped,* she told herself as she turned her mind back to those stunning dark curls. *You will be mine! All mine!*

She was sure she was going to faint during the break when they all descended on the snacks and he came around to her side of the table and whispered in her ear, asking if he could drive her home. She whispered yes to those beautiful brown curls brushing her cheek. She still didn't know his name, but that didn't matter.

It was the custom for boys to ask a girl they were interested in to drive them home in their buggy after the singing, making plenty of time to get to know one another. If this first meeting was going well, the boy could also take the back roads or the long way home to extend the date into the wee hours of the night (or morning.)

After the supper was served and cleaned up, boys were trying to find certain girls in the melee as horses were being hitched up to buggies for the ride home. Swarthy, as she was now calling him until she knew his name, had dashed around the table as everyone stood, grabbed her hand and pulled her through the crowd toward the field of buggies. He was still holding her hand as he helped her up onto the raised seat. Holding hands was usually frowned upon until a couple were engaged, signified by the marriage banns being announced in church. *He's moving pretty fast,* Sarabeth told herself. *I wonder how many girlfriends he is keeping... Well, they will all disappear when he gets to know me...*she assured herself.

Once they were on the road, he switched the reins to his left hand and again took her hand with his right. She moved in closer to him on the plush crushed velvet upholstered bench. As their shoulders touched, he turned and planted a quick kiss on her lips, leaving her utterly speechless. She had sat on hard backless benches through endless sermons over the years warning the *youngie* that they were playing with fire if they entertained any sort of affection at all before marriage. *Obviously*, she thought, *his district either didn't have similar homilies or this guy is playing with fire...or maybe he is sure I am the one...perhaps. Oh, I'll die!*

Part Three

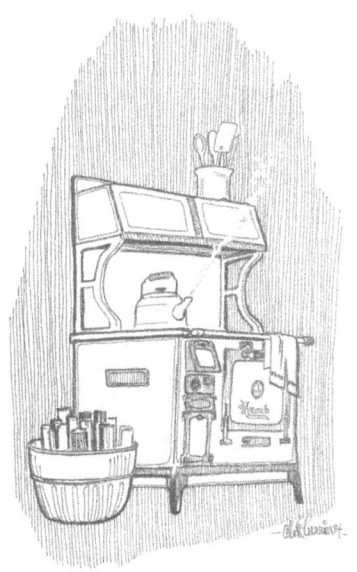

CHAPTER 29

Phoebe & Stephen

T he ride to the hospital was uneventful, though their spirits were high. Phoebe and Stephen were in the back seat, their hands entwined, their minds wondering what the day might hold for them. Well, two new babies, for sure. Mr. Schrock and *Mamm* were in the front seat, her eyes shut tight, not only to block out the landscape as it whizzed past—far faster than any buggy she had ever been in—but also deep in prayer, asking the Lord for a safe, protected journey and that they wouldn't end up in an accident going these speeds, but also for the doctors and a safe birth for her only daughter and the babies.

"Well, I guess we're batching it tonight," *Dat* said, peering into the kerosene-run refrigerator while Levi sat at the kitchen table scanning *The Budget*.

"Maybe some turkey sandwiches?" *Dat* asked.

"Sounds great," Levi answered.

"Oh, and here's some of her corn chowder soup, too. That ought to be plenty," *Dat* continued, "and what's that dessert you brought?"

"Oh, Mile-high pie. *Yo,* that'll be good," Levi agreed while still scanning the paper.

"*Yo*, listen to this one, will *ya?*" Levi began. "This is in the classifieds...these folks in Smyrna, Maine...ah...they want to know if there is anyone out there who builds buggies that are custom made for wheelchairs. I guess that would be a problem, huh? I wouldn't mind tackling that one with Stephen. Maybe we should write them back...a fold up, expandible ramp or something? And straps or clamps on the floor to secure it. It would depend on if it was for the driver or a passenger though...huh...."

They were all chatting at once when they arrived at the hospital, all wondering if they would have two boys or two girls or one of each at the end of the day. Each had silently prayed that they would all be protected, and that God's angels would surround them.

While *Mamm* sat in the waiting room at the hospital sipping her third cup of awful vending machine cocoa, Susanna and Phoebe were dozing off in their room in the maternity wing, Susanna ensconced in a Lazy Boy lounge chair, her feet in the air and her head on a pillow, a flannel hospital sheet covering most of her form and the chair besides. Phoebe was practically sitting up in bed with the head raised and her eyes closed. Stephen was spread out on the very narrow and definitely too short sofa under the window in the room, the hospital's nod to dads being allowed to stay in the room during the entire birth. While trying to fit into it comfortably, Stephen had commented that the architects of this particular bed-couch-thing must have been Little People. He settled for being on his back with his knees up, his feet flat against the opposite wall.

There had been a bustle of activity when they'd first arrived. Checking in, blood samples, blood pressure checks, monitors, and Dopplers to listen to the babies had all made the first two hours in the hospital fly by. All the nurses were hoping the babies would be born on their shift, but it appeared these babies just might have other ideas. There had been no spontaneous contractions since her water broke back home on the farm, so the doctor felt there was no problem waiting while Phoebe caught up on some sleep, for now at least.

A nurse tiptoed into the room and silently took Phoebe's blood pressure. Phoebe opened her eyes.

"Are they okay?" she ventured.

"Everything looks really good. Try to sleep. We don't have to hurry anything along for now. We've got another forty-eight hours before we'll worry about getting things going. Your water broke less than eight hours ago, so we've got plenty of time. No need to rush it," the nurse assured her.

I am so ready to be done being pregnant, Phoebe thought to herself. *I can't believe we'll be holding them soon. I wonder how hard labor will really be. The three births I've been to at school were all so different, and each mom reacted so differently. I'm nervous, but not scared.* Her midwife, Roberta, had been so reassuring, saying, "Your body has grown these little guys and I promise you it knows how to get them out too." *Doubting Thomas,* she thought to herself. *Oh, ye of little faith!*

She slipped into a sound sleep then and barely stirred while nurses came and went during the night.

At 4:00 a.m. the first contraction hit like a runaway truck. "OWWWWWW!" Phoebe howled. Susanna and Stephen each opened one eye, not sure if they had been dreaming or if this was the real thing.

"AGH!" was the next expletive escaping Phoebe's lips. Susanna leaped up, catching her feet between the chair and the footrest, until she wiggled herself free and rushed to the bed to hold Phoebe's hand, pressing the emergency call light on the wall at the head of the bed on her way.

The contraction eased slightly and then disappeared.

"Now, you'll never have to do that one again," she assured her. "Just rest until the next one. Then breathhhhheee... that's it. You are doing great! You got this girl!" Susanna encouraged.

"You can cut out the cheerleader stuff, Susanna," Phoebe growled and looked at her sideways. "It doesn't suit you. And no loud counting later. I hate that. Just quiet so I can concentrate, okay?"

Phoebe was quickly transferred into the delivery suite across the hall while Stephen and Susanna followed.

"Yup. Okay," Susanna whispered her promise. "No cheer-leading."

"Do you want me to rub your back or your stomach?" Stephen asked hopefully. "Feet?"

Through gritted teeth, Phoebe said, "Don't...touch...me..." as she tried to get the hang of breathing slowly while being hit with a train this time. Her nails dug into his arm as she squeezed, trying to hang on for dear life.

"You really are doing great," Susanna whispered after the contraction passed. At that very moment, the room filled up with people: nurses, doctors, neonatal specialists pushing two infant warmers, and an anesthetist with her assistant should they need to go to plan B if the babies didn't tolerate labor well. Two teams had been designated, each assigned to either Baby A, the first one appearing, or Baby B who until now was higher up in her uterus.

As another contraction ramped up, Phoebe closed her eyes and remembered her imaging exercises. Every night before bed, while she waited for sleep to overtake her, she had breathed slowly and tried to imagine the birth how she hoped it would be. The room would be perfectly quiet. Her eyes would be closed like this so she could concentrate. She would ride each rush (a nicer word than contraction) like a huge ocean swell, breathing in as it built and then breathing out as it petered out on the downside. Over and over until her babies wiggled down and she would push first one and then the other out into the world.

"Try to rest between each rush," Susanna suggested. With her eyes still closed, Phoebe instantly fell asleep only to wake up about three minutes later when the next rush started cresting.

The nurse at the foot of the bed announced a bit too loudly, "There is no cord present, and you are at seven centimeters!"

"Shhhhh," Phoebe admonished. "I don't need to know that."

Everyone in the room was in their assigned spot, frozen as if in a game of Mother May I? One nurse sat at a monitor on the far side of the room gently tapping the keyboard while documenting the labor's progress. You could even hear the clock ticking. The

Doppler has been turned down, but they could still hear the low *blub blub* of at least one of the heartbeats.

Ten minutes went by. Fifteen. Then all of a sudden Phoebe's eyes flew open and she announced, "I am going to push!" and with that the doctor tapped on the shoulder of the nurse sitting at the end of the bed. She silently jumped up and he sat down in her place.

Roberta walked in at that moment and came to the side of the bed opposite Stephen taking Phoebe's free hand in hers. "I told you they'd tell you when they are ready, dear," she whispered.

"Baby's crowning!" the doctor announced while still situating himself on the little wheeled stool, failing in his attempt to say that quietly.

"Okay, Phoebe," he said in a lower tone. "Pant slowly now... that's it..." he said as he checked for a cord around the baby's neck before the shoulders would descend.

"Another push now..." he suggested, though he amended that comment by saying, "when the next contraction comes..."

The baby's head was out, and the doctor wiped away any fluid on his face while waiting for the next rush.

"Catch the dad!" the anesthesiologist called from the head of the bed. A male nurse with shiny black dreadlocks standing behind Stephen caught him as he fainted and lowered him to the floor. He quickly recovered and stood up, though looking quite pale still. The male nurse leaned over and whispered to Stephen, "You don't need to hold your breath, bro,'" while offering him a chair.

When the next rush finally came, and everyone in the room could breathe again—they had been holding their breaths too— the slippery little guy barreled out into the doctor's hands with a loud howl of protest against this very new, very uncomfortable situation he found himself in after nine months of dark, warm cozy bliss.

"It's a boy!" Stephen announced. "Pheebs, it's a boy!" he practically yelled.

"And...there's...another...one...still," Phoebe said slowly with her eyes still closed, determined to stay calm, knowing her work wasn't over yet, not by a long shot. She briefly dozed while the rest of the room scurried around. Stephen was handed a pair of sterile surgical scissors and instructed to cut the cord. He didn't faint this time.

The pudgy pink boy continued to holler. He was not happy, not approving of this new situation a bit.

"Here," a nurse said to Phoebe as she handed over the baby now wrapped in a little flannel blanket. "He wants you." Phoebe opened her eyes and stared at the little pink person in her arms.

"It is unbelievable. Stephen, he's here. Can you believe it?" she whispered.

"I know. You did it, Pheebs. You did it!" he said.

"Here you take him," she said suddenly frowning. "I'm having another rush."

"Don't push yet, just pant," the doctor instructed, quietly this time. Then he assured her, "There's no cord. You can push when you feel like it."

Six minutes later, the second baby slid out, silently blinking at all the bright lights as if asking what planet she had just landed on.

"Is it another boy?" Stephen asked.

"No," the doctor said. "You have a girl."

"But that is the *least* likely combination seeing as we don't have any twins in either of our families," Phoebe puzzled philosophically as Baby Boy A began howling again. "Stephen," she said, looking for him in the crowd around her bed. "We don't even have a girl's name picked out!"

Stephen took the baby girl, now also swaddled in an identical receiving blanket to her brother's while a nurse handed Baby Boy back to Phoebe. As if on cue, both babies started wailing their protests. The entire room echoed with their cries while everyone started laughing. The hospital personnel began leaving as they packed up their equipment. These two little ones were doing just fine and wouldn't be needing any help here.

When there was finally room, Phoebe's mother tentatively walked to the side of the bed. She had been ushered in by a nurse in time to see both babies being born.

"Oh my!" was all she could say at first. "Oh my! They are just beautiful! Look at you little guys! I was absolutely putrified something was gonna go wrong. I was beside myself. Thank you, Jesus! And you are both okay. Better than okay. Praise the Lord! How much do they weigh, Phoebe?"

"We haven't weighed them yet," Phoebe answered. "I wanted to wait. We actually have all day. I just want them close for now. I wrote it all in our birth plan so everyone else was on board. But, um, *Mamm*, I think you mean 'PET-rified', *eh?*"

Mamm addressed the baby boy she was now holding while plainly ignoring Phoebe. "There she goes again. See, she thinks she's so smart, correcting me even here. Well, kiddo, we'll show her. Won't we?" She continued talking to the baby who was almost asleep then.

Stephen pulled a chair up to the bed where *Mamm* could sit and hold him.

"How can you even write a birth plan if you have no idea how it will all go?" *Mamm* turned back to Phoebe.

Phoebe explained, "We had certain wishes, but we were always open to changing things if anything came up that we weren't expecting, like if the second baby flipped and decided to come breech—feet first—but it all went pretty smoothly I'd say."

"This one is going into Bolivian..." *Mamm* said, studying the little face. Phoebe didn't even try to correct her, but looked at Stephen and whispered, "I think she means 'oblivion'" and shook her head laughing. When all the excitement had settled down, and the babies were tucked in side by side in the little glass isolette and sound asleep, and the family had eaten supper in the room, it was time for *Mamm* and Susanna to head home. Mr. Schrock had been called and would be at the hospital soon. *Mamm* wrapped her shawl around herself, her purse on her arm and stood at the end of the bed with her head slightly tilted studying Phoebe. "*Ya* know," she began. "We didn't even ask what their names are."

"Oh dear," said Phoebe. Stephen stepped up then. "We like Naomi for a girl—you'd said that Pheebes, remember?—and Mattanya for a boy." Phoebe nodded, smiling.

Mamm asked, "What kinda' name is that?" as she scowled.

"It means '*Gott's* gift,'" Stephen explained. "Naomi was Ruth's mother's name in the Bible. It means 'pleasantness.'"

"Well, I can live with that I s'pose," *Mamm* said, still frowning. "I'll just call him 'Matty.' I wouldn't remember the other way to say it.

"They might make fun of that in school, *ya* know," she added.

"Well," Stephen began. "There are lots of interesting names popping up in all the settlements. What about Zillah and Moab over in Wisconsin? Or I recently saw Boaz and Gaius from that family that just had their second set of twins in Ohio?"

Phoebe added, "In school there is a Joah, a Keturah, an Omri, a Tirzah, and a Zipporah. Biblical names are unique in the U.S. but common elsewhere in the world, like Boaz, Linus, and Adah. I've been collecting names for a while now," she informed them.

"So, all of our grandchildren will have odd names, then?" *Mamm* asked suspiciously.

"You'll have to wait and see, I guess," Stephen said. "Let's just get these little guys going first, okay?" He was exhausted from all the excitement. Susanna took her cue from Stephen and ushered *Mamm* out, saying, "I bet the car is here already."

Stephen kissed Phoebe goodnight before placing a gently kiss on each baby's head. He looked back at Phoebe then as he again tried to fold himself into the sofa-shelf-bed thing under the window. Pulling up a flannel blanket around himself, he added, "I hope we know what we've gotten ourselves into."

"Too late now," Phoebe replied with her eyes closed. "Better get some sleep while they're out," she counselled. "They'll be ready to nurse in a couple of hours. Just saying."

"Lord help us," Stephen mused.

CHAPTER 30

Sarabeth

Swarthy followed Sarabeth's directions to the end of the long gravel driveway at Faith and Noah's farm. Stopping at the bottom of the drive, he halted the horse. Turning toward her, he wrapped her in a tight embrace and proceeded to kiss her passionately. She didn't even try to resist, but returned the hug and simply melted into his strong arms and chest as his hands began roaming below her neck. The perfume hadn't missed his notice, either.

"You're cute," he finally said when he came up for air after the last kiss.

"I love you," she responded.

"Whoa," he said as he pulled back, sitting up straighter on the padded bench. He placed his hands on her shoulders and looked deep into her eyes, his mind racing. *Whoa, bro,'* he told himself. *Careful now. This one is trouble...like that last chick back in Ohio was. And I am not interested in a shotgun wedding. No, sir. I got out of that one by the skin of my teeth when she wouldn't tell them who the father was that time. This one is even flakier, I'm reckoning.*

Somebody's prayers were certainly with Sarabeth on this buggy ride that night. She had no idea what she was dealing with, lacking neither the maturity or experience to discern people as of yet. Her choices could have affected the entire rest of her life, complicating things beyond her wildest imagination, and damaging her future relationships.

His hands were sweating as he realized she was moving in for another kiss, ready to abandon all common sense, it appeared. He had read her correctly. *No way, you're not going there,* he told himself. *Nope. I've learned my lesson. How do I let her down softly? Don't need this one following me around town now...and I don't want to have to run off again and disappear like last time...though I might have to, I'm guessing. Stupid! That's what I am. I thought I'd just have a bit of fun tonight, but no, I pick a basket case. I thought I'd found an easy catch... didn't learn my lesson, I s'pose...*

"Listen, then," he began. "It's late. They're gonna wonder where you are, and I have to catch an early train in a few hours. I'm contracted to work in Montana next, a big job. I'm sorry, but I'll have to keep in touch then," he said as he jumped out of the buggy and ran around to her side, flinging the door open, and lifted her out, setting her on her feet on the road. He had to say something, anything. He hesitated as he dusted off his hands, as if he could wipe away this nightmare before him like powder.

"It's been fun," he said as he ran back to the driver's side of the buggy and jumped in, grabbing the reins and taking off before Sarabeth even had time to answer him. She pulled her shawl around herself tighter as she watched the buggy race back down the road until it was out of sight. It didn't dawn on her what he had implied. Her goofy smile was still stuck in place. It didn't even occur to her yet that she had been literally taken for a ride. All she knew was that she was in love and had found her prince. Exactly like in the fairy tales.

Levi was just cutting a second piece of the Mile-high sweet potato pie for both of them when *Mamm* and Susanna came in through the back kitchen door, both talking at once.

"Well, *Dat*, we have two of the most beautiful grandbabies you have ever seen and a boy and a girl! I couldn't believe it. And they are healthy and everyone is fine, praise *Gott!* But boy, can they howl!" *Mamm* exclaimed, laughing as she wiggled out of her shawl and going-to-town shoes.

"I couldn't hear myself think over that din," Susanna added.

"Pie to celebrate?" *Dat* offered.

"*Yo,*" Susanna said.

"Me too. You work up an appetite standing around that place doin' nothing, for sure," *Mamm* marveled as she put the coffee pot on the gas range.

"They are the cutest little things ever," *Mamm* added.

"They aren't that little though," Susanna reminded her. "They were each just under eight pounds the midwife is guessing. They'll weight them later tonight, I am sure."

"*Ya* know, Susanna, they don't even look alike. The little girl's face is kind of scrunched up a bit and the little boy has this big nose like his *doddy,* I'm guessing. And she has a bit of dark hairs and he is a blondie. Definitely a blondie," *Mamm* said as she and Susanna sat down at the table and dug into their pie.

CHAPTER 31
Naomi & Mattanya

G raduation was upon them. The Four Musketeers had made it to the finish line along with only a handful of their schoolmates, five others to be exact. It had been a comprehensive course, preparing them for nursing work wherever they chose to go. Their being members of Plain congregations certainly limited their choices going forward. None would abandon their church in favor of a job elsewhere, but they considered this when they first agreed to join the nursing program. They would be ostracized should they leave against the advice of the church, some even shunned, but the original purpose of this radical step was to enhance the care of their own people. It was already bearing fruit at home and in the wider community, and the four girls certainly felt honored to have been asked to serve in this way. It had been a very full two years of learning and growing. The rest of their lives surely held the promise of using their new skills, through many opportunities.

Hilda wasn't getting married until the end of August, so she had signed up for an introduction to the RN program being offered during the summer semester. She could do so much more as a registered nurse and see if there was a specialty she felt drawn to. One option was midwifery, though she didn't know if she really wanted to go to school for three more years, especially with the prospect of children coming along once they were married.

Phoebe and Stephen brought the babies to the graduation ceremony and reception afterward and were swamped by their friends wanting to get a good look at little Naomi and Mattanya. Hilda, Susanna and Leah had all been able to visit them at the farm after they came home from the hospital three weeks ago.

The class assembled on the stage, sans babies, toward the end of the ceremony. The teachers called each of the nine girls who had remained in the program till the end by name. Each then came up to the podium to be pinned, receiving that precious little lapel LPN symbol representing numerous hours and months of hard work, and yes, blood—literally—sweat and tears. At the calling of each girl's name, family and friends in the audience cheered, whistled, clapped and hooted from the assembly hall below the stage.

The little family was the highlight of the reception, being fussed over with offers to hold each of the babies. Of course, there was the odd student or a parent present who asked, 'but are they identical?' to which Stephen or Phoebe gave their pat answer: "yup," knowing they would have to figure that out on their own...or not. They were obviously dressed one in a pink onesie and the other in a blue onesie, those little one-piece outfits—Stephen called the baby bodysuits 'chicken skins'—but that didn't deter the questions.

On the way home after the reception, in Mr. Schrock's borrowed SUV taxi, with both babies buckled into the back seat with Phoebe wedged in between them, Stephen in the front passenger seat, and *Mamm* and *Dat* in the third seat behind Phoebe and the sleeping babies, *Mamm* continued to marvel that Phoebe had indeed graduated.

"What will you do with yourself now that you are done with school?" *Mamm* wanted to know.

Stephen answered for them, "Well, learn how to take care of these two and be parents, for one."

Phoebe answered next. "And try to get a bit of sleep. I can't believe how tired I am!"

"They're still up at night?" *Dat* asked.

"Well, *ya*," Phoebe answered. "Most nights I bring them into *die gute schtup* to feed them, so they don't wake up Stephen. They still want to play then, wide awake for hours. I try to nap with them in the morning after Stephen leaves, but that is usually only an hour or so."

Dat was quiet for a minute and then asked, "but do you light the lamps in the living room when you're in there?"

"Well, *ya*. Why?" she wanted to know.

"Well," he began. "They probably think it's time to get up then. Maybe turn off the lamps and they'll go back to sleep," he suggested.

"Duh. Why I didn't think of that? *Dat,* when did you turn into Dr. Spock?" Phoebe asked, shaking her head.

"Oh, we had a couple of night owls too. We finally figured it out, right, *Mamm*?" he answered, chuckling.

"That made all the difference," *Mamm* replied. "They grow up so fast. I never believed it when people told me that. I thought I'd be swamped with babies and diapers coming out of my ears forever, with no light at the end of the funnel and the next thing you know they're going to school and then they're playing on the outhouse roof and then they're courting and then they have families of their own. Just enjoy them while they're little," was *Mamm's* sage advice. "Trust me on this one," she added. Phoebe let *Mamm's* last slip go, but just smiled at Stephen, who hadn't missed it either.

CHAPTER 32
Susanna & Leah

S usanna and Levi were very happily married. Marital bliss is the term. The Hutterian colony had risen to the occasion of their very first nurse getting married and pulled out all the stops for that wedding, and only a few months after that graduating with her LPN license also became the focus of further festivities, school performances, hilarious skits and celebrating. She was kept busy, actually excused from having a cook week like all the other under-forty-five *basels* because she was soon snatched up not only with her own community's medical needs and questions but also being invited to other *'hofs* to get her opinion on a whole myriad of concerns that many of the *mudders* there had.

They'd never felt comfortable with the doctor and his condescending ways and inflated invoices—some said he was downright evil—that served most of the colonies in the county, ending up avoiding health care all together, hoping and praying the problems would magically go away. Not the best prescription for most maladies. They'd often end up in the emergency room with an illness that could have been treated so much sooner, avoiding all that worry and suffering.

Levi would drive her to the far-reaching borders of the colonies, some so isolated the only outsiders who ever visited besides Hutterite families from other *'hofs* were the vet when he was called to consult on one of the animals, or delivery trucks bringing orders to the farms or workshops. While Susanna visited with the *basels,* he would seek out the *vetters* in their designated work departments and catch up on all the news there.

Each community was essentially self-sufficient. The *vetters*—the men also called 'the brothers'—often drove down to Minneapolis, or up to Fargo or Sioux Falls, or Milwaukee for their bulk shopping, building supplies and paint and various other purchases, making visitors to the colonies even rarer. Sometimes a few of the *basels* would ride along and get dropped off at fabric warehouses to stock up on material and notions for the coming year, or Savers or Goodwill thrift stores. A trip to the city was also the perfect occasion to eat out at a restaurant after shopping, a very rare treat indeed.

Each colony had a fabric room that was overseen by one of the older sisters. The sewing room sister was responsible for making sure that there was enough cloth for all of the clothing required by the growing families under her care. There were baby clothes to make, underthings for men and women, trousers, shirts and dresses and the traditional scarves for women. The dress material had to have enough of a range of colors to satisfy all of the women and also to be considered was the fact that the older sisters preferred less showy colors and patterns compared to the younger women who might still be looking to attract a husband. The sisters also made all of their bed linens, their curtains, quilts and winter wear: hooded parkas in all sizes from toddlers to the elderly, and quilted work vests that had recently hit an all-time high approval rating among the *vetters.* Many *'hofs* can also boast a cobbler shop where custom shoes, boots, and horse tack are still made to this day.

The *vetters* would also bring along a grocery list from the head cook with all the items they couldn't grow or can or make at home. Occasionally, a few interesting or even exotic items would turn up after these shopping trips. Recently, several grocery bags of assorted Oriental vegetables and condiments appeared. It turned out that a certain brother had a wish for Chinese food that he had fallen in love with at a restaurant on a previous trip. The sisters were completely at a loss as to how to prepare all of it, much less for over one hundred people who would descend on the dining room later that day. After scanning old copies of *The Budget* without any results there (Maudie must not know how to cook chow mien) they did actually find several Asian offerings in both *The Joy of Cooking* and *Betty Crocker's Cookbook*.

Susanna and Levi were home the day the special dinner was served. The effusive prayer at the end of the meal reflected the elder brother's complete satisfaction with the culinary results:

"We THANK YOU, Father, for this DEEE-LISHOUS meal that You have provided for us. Please bless the cooks and all of us. AMEN!"

Leah and Ben were equally happy as young marrieds. Leah was also visited often by women in their community with medical questions both for themselves and their children. She had spent time meeting the health professionals in the wider medical community at the hospital and neighboring clinics and introduced herself while discussing ways she could refer patients to them. Their support was universal, and they greeted her enthusiastically, as they had often puzzled how to reach this underserved community among themselves.

She often spent the day with her mother who was caring for their *Oma* who forever appeared bright and happy. Leah was also immensely enjoying taking care of their first darling little house and the gardens surrounding it. She still woke up some mornings afraid she had forgotten to set the alarm and missed her ride to school. It would take quite a while to really believe she was done with college. She looked forward to starting a family, hoping as the weeks went by that perhaps they had actually been successful on that front.

Ben was always encouraging, reminding her that sometimes it just takes longer for some than for others. They included this wish in their prayers together every single night, trusting that God would send children in the right time. They were certainly hopeful as their own siblings and their parents as well were all apparently quite fertile. It was a mystery. And a heartache. *What if I never have babies?* Leah began to wonder. *What if something is wrong with one of us? Would Ben even consider adopting? Would we be eligible to adopt? What would the social services in our area think of us? What requirements would they have for their couples? Would we both need a college education? That will never happen. Perhaps God is punishing us for being disobedient, marrying outside of our faiths.*

But the fact was that they had been married seven months already. Each time a new month in her cycle disappointed her, she tried and failed to remain optimistic, crying into her pillow, bravely perking up when Ben came home from work. Her mother was a huge help, encouraging her to trust and believe it would happen soon. Aunts and girlfriends would hint in whispers, eager to find out if something was indeed growing already that they weren't privy to.

By the time their first anniversary was upon them, Leah was ready to get a professional opinion on this baby-making business. Being obsessed with it and constantly frustrated wasn't helping at all. Ben deserved a happier wife. It was time to figure this out. She made an appointment with a midwife in the next town on a day she usually went shopping there, anyway.

The midwife could find nothing obviously wrong but suggested an infertility workup with a gynecologist she recommended. It felt encouraging just to be doing *something*. The midwife also suggested Leah take and chart her temperature every morning, which would help determine the exact time of ovulation. They could understand their fertile times better that way. By 'trying' as soon as her period ended each month, they could conceivably (no pun intended) be using up viable sperm before the best days were even beginning in her cycle. She listed further options that the couple could also explore should they not find any answers there. Leah left her office far happier than she had been in a while. Maybe there was hope.

CHAPTER 33

Ivan & Hilda

Dear Ivan,

I have been thinking. I could take those extra courses and work toward an RN, but maybe, perhaps, there are other ways we could serve. It occurred to me the other night at prayer that while we are young, before children start coming along, we could do a stint in the foreign missions. Together after we are married in August. Have you ever considered that? It would be terribly exciting, don't you think? We could be sent anywhere in the world and maybe make a difference. With my LPN and your skills, I can imagine we'd get through the screening process pretty easily. Please tell me what your thoughts might be. I can't wait to see you again. When can you come this way next, hopefully before the wedding? I can't wait that long.

With all my love and prayers,
Hilda

Dearest Hilda,

God works in strange ways. The same thought came to me at work this week. Do you think we are being led? It is hard to call it coincidence. Some call it 'God-incidence.' I could contact Mennonite Central Committee and kind of get a feel for the lay of the land in this direction, see if we'd fit the requirements, see what countries are asking for mission-

aries. It is very exciting. My parents were in India for many years, even after their first children were born. There was a boarding school for the kids of all the missionaries and they didn't get to see their parents except for major holidays and summer break. I am not sure I would want to repeat that, but it would be one of my questions to them. We could be sent anywhere. Do you have any preferences? Wishes? I would love to see South America. I worked in Mexico once, rebuilding a clinic on a hilltop, clearing the road of rocks for weeks. I also got to go to Pakistan for three months after those earthquakes in August 2005. We put up aluminum shelters. Some aid groups had put up tents, but those wouldn't last through the winter, so we changed direction and installed the huts with stone fire pits in them for cooking and warmth. The tent thing hadn't been researched enough.

A bunch of my friends went to New Orleans that same August when Hurricane Katrina hit the coast in 2005. Habitat for Humanity was kept busy down there rebuilding for years after that.

I just looked MCC up and there is a seed project opening in Zambia and MCC Ukraine is asking for folks too. SWAP (Sharing With Appalachian People) in the U.S. is begging for people. It also looks like they have programs with Indigenous Inuit peoples in Alaska. Can you imagine? "The harvest is plentiful, but the workers are few."

I'm going to read more and will let you know what I find. It's terribly exciting. We just have to pray that this is God's will for us, and not ours. It will only bear fruit if it is.

With all my love,

Ivan

CHAPTER 34

Faith

Faith had gone to bed at midnight after trying to stay up for Sarabeth to return home after the singing. She figured she'd had a good time and would be home soon. She knew the *boova*—the boys who were working on her farm—would look after her; she had specifically asked them to since Sarabeth was new to the area.

When Faith woke in the morning, she quietly went down to the kitchen. Sure enough, Sarabeth's shoes were on the mat at the back door and her shawl was also there hung on a peg. Faith guessed she would probably sleep in since it was a no-church Sunday. She would go about the morning chores with Baby Patience close by until Sarabeth appeared.

Faith was surprised to hear a buggy rattle up the driveway so early. She looked out and saw that it was Phoebe's *mamm* and *dat*. They certainly had not been asked to keep her company since Sarabeth had come. With Patience propped up on one hip, she held the back door open for them to enter.

"*Gut* morning!" Phoebe's *mamm* said. "I brought along some of Maudie's famous breakfast pizza. If you've eaten already, you can always warm it up for later today, too."

"Why, *denke*. That sounds *wunderbar*. That is a surprise." Faith said, taking the tray and gingerly setting it on the sideboard. "Can I put on some coffee?"

"No, not for us. We just had ours," *Dat* answered.

They sat down at the table after *Mamm* took Patience on her lap.

"She's growing, isn't she?" *Mamm* asked, trying to fill the awkward silence.

"She is," Faith answered, trying to sound cheerful and not suspicious.

"Well," *Dat* began. "Your *dat* received a letter a while back that he shared with me." He stopped and looked at Faith, trying to judge if she was listening or becoming defensive already. He really didn't know how she would react.

"Well, I'll make this simple. We've all been so glad how you've managed after the accident. It's been a long road. We all appreciate that. But all of us that care so much about you are wondering if maybe you've thought about marrying again."

At that, *Mamm* spoke. "If it were me, I'd have put that thought out of my mind for good, but you are so young and have so many *gut* years left. Plus the whole farm to care for. We'd like to help you out here too, if it's *Gott's* will."

"I'm not ready for that," Faith stated plainly.

Mamm was quick to answer her. "No, I don't think anyone is ever ready after what you've been through, but we want to help you to start to think about it. There's no great rush. You'd want to get to know him first and take your time."

"You mean you know who I should get to know? You're matchmaking?" Faith asked, horrified. This was the farthest thing from her mind. How could they even suggest it?

Dat answered. "There are some wonderful brothers out there who have lost their wives like you've lost Noah. There is one in Canada that the bishop there wrote to your *dat* about. He is your age, not some old widower. His wife was only thirty-five when she died of cancer. And they have *kinner.*" He let that sink in for a moment.

Faith was twisting the corner of her apron, looking down in her lap. Tears were streaming down her cheeks. Finally, she spoke.

"You mean a marriage of convenience?" she said as she looked up at *Mamm* and *Dat* and stated angrily, "he needs a *mamm* and I need someone to run my farm? I could never do that. *No!*"

"I am not implying that," *Dat* was quick to explain. "No, a marriage should be based on *Gott* and on love first. But sometimes love grows, too, as you get to know each other."

"And sometimes it doesn't and you're stuck for the rest of your life in hell. No! Never," she said as she covered her face with her hands and sobbed. They all took a moment to breathe in then.

"I didn't think about it really," Faith finally said, feeling she had no choices anymore, that she had only imagined she'd moved on since the accident. People decided things for her back then, and it was starting all over again now. "I thought I should be true to Noah for the rest of my life. I can't imagine, you know," here she looked over at *Mamm*, "speaking intimately with someone else, loving anyone else. But it's done...by some...isn't it? Wow," she said, taking a deep breath. "I need to pray about this, okay? I don't need to decide today, do I?" she asked, feeling completely defeated.

"Absolutely not," *Dat* answered gently. Just then, Sarabeth came down the stairs, curious to see who was visiting so early. Faith quickly wiped any lingering tears away with the back of her hand, hoping Sarabeth hadn't heard what they had been talking about.

"Morning, Sarabeth," *Dat* said. "Sleeping in? Is Faith driving you so hard now?"

"*Ach,* no. It's been great. I was just up late. I went to the singing. It was *gut* fun."

Then *Mamm* spoke as she stood up. "Well, we'd better be getting on and let you two have your breakfast."

Dat stood up and squished Patience's chubby cheeks, which made her giggle and *Dat* smile.

"Take care now," *Dat* said, and looking at Faith he added, "We'll talk again, okay?"

She nodded, taking Patience back from *Mamm*.

The End

Coming Summer 2023

The Pearl of Great Price, The Amish Nurse Series, Book 4

———————————

Don't miss out on your next favorite book!

Join the Satin Romance mailing list
www.satinromance.com/mail.html

Acknowledgments

I have given birth to a series of books full of true stories and memories gathered from a lifetime of amazing encounters with other cultures and diverse peoples. Firstly, I want to thank my sister, the real Phebe Schwartz—yes, spelled without an 'o'--for the amazing job she did editing all the books in the series. I also want to thank my very own personal research assistant and librarian, Rosalyn Hope for her hours of hunting down every last one of my endless requests.

I also owe a great debt to the mothers and babies I have had the privilege of serving for so many years and all I learned from each one: Amish *mamms*, Hutterite *mueters*, Hmong *nias*, Vietnamese, Somali, Ethiopian, Native American and all the other brave women I have met. Many thanks go to my Canadian Hutterite *basel*-friend who advised me when it came to *Hutterische* language and culture. Special thanks go to my dear friend and author, Phyllis Moore for her love, prayers, and support. I also owe a great debt of gratitude to WOW (Women of Words) and NLW/RWA (Northern Lights Writers/ Minnesota chapter of Romance Writers of America,) and Patricia Morris (past president of MIPA, Minnesota Independent Publishers Association) all author-friends who have so unselfishly shared their wisdom and experience of the writing and publishing world with me. I couldn't have done this without each one of you! And last but not least, my courageous prayer partner, Tabatha. You have no idea.

I want to especially thank my own midwife, Nancy Schumacher and her brilliant team at Melange Books who were my midwives and doulas throughout the birthing of my books in the Amish Nurse Series. Also, I want to thank my most vocal critics, Alexsi Currier and his wife Anastasia for reading the drafts and keeping me on my toes throughout the long months of the Pandemic. Of course, I can't end without expressing my eternal gratitude to my dearest husband of 47 years, David, and my children, Abraham, Isaac, Ruth, Rachel, and Hannah Rose for their undying love, encouragement and support no matter how crazy mother's latest creation appears to be.

A Note from the Author

I've been asked what I am writing now.

The next series after the four Amish Nurse books that are now being published, is also an Amish romance saga. Some of your favorite characters from the first series might reappear, others will continue to live happily ever after and ride off into the sunset in their horse-drawn buggies. I hope to again capture the very essence of Amish faith and values while navigating the reality in our world of spiritual struggles, dashed hopes, innumerable challenges that everyday life has in store for us and disappointment. There are always the answers to prayers to find intense joy in, and the beauty of His innumerable blessings too.

THANK YOU FOR READING

Did you enjoy this book?

We invite you to leave a review at the website of your choice, such as Goodreads, Amazon, Barnes & Noble, etc.

DID YOU KNOW THAT LEAVING A REVIEW...

- Helps other readers find books they may enjoy.
- Gives you a chance to let your voice be heard.
- Gives authors recognition for their hard work.
- Doesn't have to be long. A sentence or two about why you liked the book will do.

About the Author

Midwife-turned-author, Stephanie Schwartz seems to swim seamlessly through cultures, religions, superstitions, raw fear and ecstasy to the first breath of a new baby. She knows how birth works and invites her readers to join her, taking us on a tour to the innermost workings of another world while giving us a rare, intimate glimpse into her daily life. She has five children scattered around the world, grandchildren, and over a thousand babies she calls her own. After writing three books on birth, and then retiring as a midwife, she realized she had most likely been in more Amish bedrooms—as a midwife—than most other authors of Amish romance novels and began researching the genre.

Thanks to the Pandemic she was able to produce the novels in the Amish Nurse Series.

facebook.com/authorstephanieschwartz

newamishromance@yahoo.com

Also by Stephanie Schwartz

The Amish Nurse Series
Worry Ends Where Faith Begins
Time Will Tell
Playing on the Outhouse Roof
The Pearl of Great Price (Coming Summer 2023)

www.ingramcontent.com/pod-product-compliance
Lightning Source LLC
Chambersburg PA
CBHW071311200626

46813CB00015B/1463